TOYCO PUBLISHING PRESENTS

HOOD
Games

A NOVEL BY
TOYLIN SIMONE

I Dedicate this book to God.

Through You all things are possible.

My Loving Parents

Luisa "Luki" Gaudino and Frank Henry

I Love You Mom and Dad

R.I.P.

ACKNOWLEDGEMENTS

My Grandma Doris you are my heart thank you for always believing in me all my life. I love you so much Mema forever and ever my Dottie xoxo.

My Grandma Sixta Gaudino Bendicion (RIP). Auntie Odette, I love you with my heart always and forever thank you for teaching me how to be strong and making me smile on cloudy days. I learned so much from you through your editing career and I am so happy I followed through love you dearly auntie RIP).

Love you Titi Rosa you hold a special place in my heart always (RIP).

My Uncles Tommy and Freddy. Uncles Murt and Bobby and Isaac. Aunt Francis, Aunt Horty, Cousin Cory and Poochie. I love you all may you continue to rest in heavenly peace god bless...

My Beautiful Sisters Nika and Tequan Friends come and go but sisters are forever. Thank you for always being by my side no matter what I love you 4 life xoxo.

My sister Kimyatta, I love you Kim keep your head up xoxo. My Bro John Bowens and Nephew Tarik I love you 4life.

Author Elle Welch and Solomon Welch, thank you so much for everything you rock.

Author Nicole Coley Shepard you are so talented and a great graphic artist I love your work you are amazing thank you xoxo.

Love you so much Troy Casey stay up xoxo.

Gerald Prince Miller love you always xoxo.

To My Gaudino and Bye Family I love you all xoxo. My Beautiful Children Taliya, Jordan and Fendi You Inspire Me Every Day Mommy Loves You Xoxoxo.

Barry Gray xoxo. S/O to Baisley Projects, 40 PJ's and Rochdale Village. My Fam! True Carter, Kezia, Jill, Renee, Nookie, Jessica, Tyrell, Lizzette and many more xoxo.

Ms. Tracy, Ms. Sheila and Ms. Dott the world needs more friends like you thanks for being a true friend xoxo.

My Girl Sadaya miss you boo love you with my heart xo. Tyrone Chandler thanks so much for the support much love.

Uncle Forest and Aunt Jiton xoxo. God Mom and Dad Jade and Frank love you.

S/O to Malik Ali you have inspired me greatly as I traveled through my journey. I really want to thank you for being such a great inspiration much love my friend Bang Out.

S/O to GMV #1 DJ Thanks so much for all the support Love You Grand Master Vic! To All My Friends and Family Much Love.

S/O to All Hustlers Grinding Hard Making Shit Happen! Believe in Yourself Every Step of the way, Get Yours, Keep Rising and Never Give Up! "Queens Stand Up Peace!!"

THE *Struggle*

"Many men are buried alive in a system behind the walls of jails, holes and prisons. and Many women are locked in cages of their mind behind the scars of struggle, pain and religion".

LIFE...

Sometimes life brings unexpected changes into your environment that may scar you in ways that a knife, gun or blade never can. Cutting and burning deeply, like a flesh wound covered in salt. The great thing about these changes, are the lessons that you learn. Sometimes your struggles and misfortunes are your best teachers. Within every setback is the opportunity for a major comeback. Take care of your inner ability to make it through any giving situation. Every experience good or bad is a great one. Sometimes life is a bowl of fuck ups sending you into a spiraling crazy war path with yourself and everyone you encounter. The beautiful thing about these fuck ups are the days you get to spend with yourself alone capturing all faults ways and actions and delivering yourself from all evil. What a lovely thing to be able to undergo so much pain and remain happy within. The mirror can be a scary place if you're not connected to your own reflection. You must search deep within to seek the true value of your essence. The worst thing you can do to yourself is run away from your truth and build a life full of lies, hate, deceit and rejection. Embrace your experiences, you are beautifully human. and Life is a great gift so keep your head held high and live it to the best of your ability.

FRANKIE

CHAPTER
one

"What a beautiful sight to see. I couldn't have picked a better place to celebrate my last week as a single man." Frankie grinned, talking to his uncle as he danced to the music while awaiting his drink at the bar. As Frankie danced, the bartender handed him a double shot of Jack Daniels with an ice-cold glass of Coca-Cola on the side. The breeze made the palm trees dance prettily in the wind, everything was perfect!

"Pay attention Frankie, everything you do, big or small requires, your undivided attention," Frankie's uncle shouted firmly. "From one kilo of cocaine, you can get up to 1-1/3 kilos. Anything more than that is no good." Frankie's uncle Bobby spoke very clearly as he walked with Frankie to the deck explaining some key factors of the drug game to his nephew. Everyone at the party was in great spirits; grinding and dancing to the music, having a good ole time, but for Bobby, it was business as usual.

Give it to Me Baby by Rick James played while two sexy strippers danced in the middle of a room filled with wealthy gentlemen. Frankie watched the strippers moves, bopping his head to the beat. *"How the fuck am I supposed to pay attention with tits and ass in the room."* Frankie thought to himself as the stripper shook her ass on the pole.

Bobby sat directly across from Frankie on the deck, with a Caribbean drink from the bar overlooking the black sands in Miami Beach. Bobby made sure to tell Frankie everything he needed to know about their business. "Your main objective is to keep the customers happy. So never be greedy. If other bosses or dealers want to cut their shit let them cut it. Customers want that good, raw, pure shit and we got the best product out in Harlem."

Bobby continued as he twirled his drink with the straw. "There's more than enough money to be made for years to come. If you want to succeed in this business, you've got to think, talk and dress like a business man. You must look sharp and dress well always. Your presence demands power and respect!" Frankie watched the water as his uncle kept talking. "You must stay wise to the code of these streets." "Yeah!" "That's right!" Frankie's uncle Murt added, walking in on his brother's conversation with their nephew. "A real boss follows his own vision. True leaders fear no man and never ever follow another man's footsteps." Murt stated, sipping on his cognac. The three fellas stood on the deck dapper than ever. Bobby and Murt explained everything at Frankie's bachelor party because they were about to traffic tons of drugs once they made it back to NYC. Murt shuffled his feet to the beat as he headed back over to the bar for a refill. Approaching the bar, Murt saw a beautiful brown skinned stripper that he wanted to spend money on. Beautiful brown voluptuous women were Murt's weakness. This stripper was very exotic with big brown eyes and big tits. Murt pulled out a big wad of cash and placed it into her bikini and whispered "You're coming with me." Frankie smiled as he watched his uncle put the moves on one of the strippers. He was amused by all the entertainment.

Frankie sat on the deck listening to his uncle with the look of admiration in his eyes.

Bobby uttered as he pulled out his gun and placed it on the table. 'Listen!' "This is a 'don't ask, don't tell, fuck you pay me' kind of business. Some crews will play fair but most will play dirty. But the eyes, they never lie! And Frankie, with those hazel eyes and the right suit, you're going to make a whole lot of money and get plenty pussy. Ha-ha ha ha," Bobby laughed as he dropped a few jewels in his nephew's ear. The cocaine business was booming, and it was an open house in the 80's. The customers who kept these dealers in business weren't just from the streets either. There were doctors, lawyers, business owners and people that you never expected used drugs. Buying large quantities of coke every week. They were living the life and loving every minute of it.

Standing in a huge beach house in Miami Beach at Frankie's bachelor party, Bobby and his brother Murt surprised Frankie by bringing a few of his closest relatives and friends down for the party. It was a beautiful sight to see. Frankie was smothered with lavish gifts, laughs and plenty entertainment. There were broads in bikini's everywhere, with a few strippers sniffing, drinking and even having sex on the beach.

The room with the Jacuzzi was occupied by Frankie's uncle Murt with one of the hot strippers they hired for the party. The house sat right by the water with a fantastic view. No matter where they were, Bobby always had a say so about their business and how he wanted shit done. He did a drug deal with a Columbian named Alberto before Frankie flew down for his surprise bachelor party.

3

Bobby and Murt brought several kilos of coke handled their business transactions and paid for transportation and shipments before flying back to New York. Bobby was very rough around the edges. He had a right hook that would knock a motherfucker out instantly. Practically every dealer in Harlem knew it. Bobby was very handsome with wavy silver hair like a Cuban. He had a cinnamon complexion and always dressed to perfection. This day he was wearing a cream-colored suit with beige gators that matched his beige Fedora hat and tie.

His pinky rings were filled with diamonds that flashed as he moved his hands while he talked. Bobby was serious about making bread and nothing or no one ever came between him or his money. Frankie smiled as he sipped through the straw of his drink before whispering to his uncle. "Damn Unc, we could be inside of a church and you'd still school me about dope and coke."

"You motherfucking right!" Bobby shouted with his hands on the table. "You can't let nothing stop your show. And you've got to stay ahead of the game at all times nephew."

"Listen Uncle Bobby, I get it, I'm here, you can count on me. I've learned from the best and I'm ready. The only thing that matters at this point is my family and my money. And there is only one person for me. I will never cheat on my wife! She's got my heart," Frankie stated with his hand on his chest.

Bobby replied "That's my boy, treat your wife like the Queen that she is and let no other get in between your union.

Believe me when I tell you, once this money starts rolling in, you're going to have bitches running left and right trying get in between the sheets," Bobby laughed as he held up his glass. "Cheers to you on your new journey in life with a beautiful family and wife." Bobby and Frankie toasted and hugged as they enjoyed the strippers, music and entertainment for the night.

There was nothing but love in the room. Frankie had a ton of gifts. There was a Louis Vuitton duffle bag and luggage set to match, that Frankie loved. Bobby told Frankie to guard that duffle bag with his life, throwing the duffle bag at Frankie hitting his chest. Frankie's eyes lit up once he opened the duffle bag and saw fifteen kilos of cocaine, along with ten thousand dollars, inside.

"Aww man, Unc! You are one crazy motherfucker for this." Frankie just laughed as he placed the bag behind the bar. Bobby smiled as he danced away to the music holding onto one of the sexy strippers at the beach house. Bobby's phone ring while he danced on the dance floor. "Hello," Bobby answered as he walked away towards the seating area. "Hey Bobby, I have an important message for you my friend." Antonio whispered abruptly. He continued "The Colombians from Miami Beach don't want you doing business here. Alberto received several warnings and the Moreno's are headed your way to come and shoot the place up. You need to get the fuck out of there now." Antonio shouted hanging up the phone. Leaving Bobby shocked at the other end of the receiver. Bobby couldn't believe that shit would go down at his nephew's event, but he took no chances.

He was having a great time with Frankie who drank, ate and partied all night long with his friends and uncles, celebrating before he married the love of his life. Bobby thought long and hard. *"How the fuck will I explain this shit to Frankie's mother?"* He thought for a minute about his older sister and then he set up shop so him and his people could get the fuck up out of there.

Bobby had Smith and Wesson pistols and machine guns loaded up in his trunk in the garage at the beach house. He and his brother made their way down the stairs and signaled Frankie to grab all his gifts and belongings. Frankie grabbed his duffle bag, luggage and envelopes filled with money and headed to the garage. Next thing you know, gunshots were flying everywhere with women and men getting shot up in and out of the beach house.

One of the strippers who had been dancing in the middle of the room was dead. The other strippers had scattered running for their lives. People were screaming and hollering, running in different directions, ducking and moving, dodging the bullets. Murt ran into the beach house and let off several shots hitting two of the shooters in the head before returning to the garage. He looked around in disbelief! There was no time to think about anything, they had to move and do it fast.

There were two shooters waiting out back by the garage. Frankie had just finished throwing his bags and money into the trunk and quickly headed towards the front of the truck so he could head out of the drive way. As he opened the door, one of the gun men approached Frankie from behind and shot him in his arm.

His uncle Bobby came running out from the side of the garage and popped two bullets in the shooter's chest. Murt screamed "Come on! We gotta get the fuck out of here now!" Murt helped Frankie and lifted him into the back seat of the truck.

Bobby, Murt and Frankie got away in the nick of time. Murt drove as fast as he could to the airport. While driving, Murt received a phone call from his friend Hector who owned a couple Yachts at the Marina Pier in Miami Beach. "Hello. Murt snarled driving in full speed away from the beach house. "Hey Murt." "Where are you?" "Alberto told me everything. Help is waiting for you my friend. I'll have a plane ready when you arrive, meet me over by the docks at the Marina and make it quick." Hector informed Murt sitting nervously at the docks near the airport. "I am almost there Hector thanks, I will be there shortly. Make sure that doctor is with you when we arrive." Murt replied hanging up the phone driving towards the Marina. Looking into the rearview mirror, Murt could see that Frankie was very weak and needed medical attention quick. Reaching the Marina, Both Bobby and Murt quickly carried Frankie over to one of Hector's Yacht's, sat him down and told him they were going for help. Murt whispered "You sit tight Frankie you hear, we will be right back with a doctor." Frankie held his uncle's hand as tight as he could, nodding his head up and down. Once the brothers reached the docks, Murt screamed out Hector's name making his presence known. "Did you call the medic?" Murt asked his friend Hector with great concern. "My nephew is in one of your yachts at the pier and he needs a doctor asap!" Hector quickly nodded his head, signaling the doctor he had on call for emergencies before they headed back to Frankie.

7

Frankie waited for his uncle's anxiously as he clenched his duffle bag filled with drugs and money. He was nervous and couldn't believe that his bachelor party had gotten shot up the way that it did. He was just happy to be alive for the moment. Frankie feared for his life as he sat in the yacht.

It was pouring raining as he ripped off a piece of cloth from his shirt, and tied it around his bloody arm that had gotten hit by one of the bullets fired back at the beach house. Thinking about how close he had come to death on such a special occasion and kicking himself for getting into the drug game. Being in this game you never know what's going to happen. All Frankie wanted to do at that moment, was get home safe out of harm's way before him and his uncles wound up killed or arrested.

The three got away safely and made it back to NY in one piece. After the dramatics of the bachelor party; Frankie thought it would be best to take a couple weeks off to get his head straight while his arm healed.

*　　　*　　　*　　　*　　　*　　　*

Rain was steadily falling through the clouds, dripping from the sky wetting the ground. All the dust that lay over top of the window pane was now washed cleaned.

It was a thunder storm that afternoon and the sky cried for a couple of hours before the sun appeared shining in its setting.

"Now things are surely looking up with this here picture I tell you that much," Frankie bragged talking to one of his buddies while he worked on his most recent painting creating a picture of eternal beauty. Frankie's pad was filled with laughter and joy as the smoke crept through the air from burning cigarettes and fresh cigars.

The smooth sounds of Marvin Gaye played on the radio, making love to their souls. Mood swings became tender and calm as Frankie's friends sat by passing around a bill filled with coke. Frankie, born and raised in Queens, New York was a handsome fella. Light skinned with hazel brown eyes that shined in the sun's light. He was tall and slender and wore his hair cut low. People continually complimented his style, mentioning how much he looked like Billie D. Frankie was very content and cool with his ways but was quick to flip a few wigs if anyone dealt the wrong hand. He was currently celebrating his new marriage to a beautiful woman named Lady. Before Frankie and Lady met, he was involved in a relationship with another female who had his child.

Frankie and his baby's mama never saw eye to eye and just couldn't come to terms throughout their relationship after his first child was born. He loved his daughter with all his heart and was an active parent before splitting up with her mother. Frankie made numerous attempts to see his child after their break up, but was turned away several times. He arrived at his daughter's doorstep one cold afternoon with a trunk filled with gifts in the back seat of his ride. Knocking at the door, Frankie had a strange feeling in his stomach. After standing outside for over ten minutes; Frankie's smile turned into a heartbroken frown.

His daughter's uncle answered the door screaming and hollering for him to get the fuck away from his property. Then he quickly calmed down once he saw Frankie standing at the door telling him that his daughter was taken away by child protective services due to neglect from the mother. His daughter's mother had a history of disappearing for days at a time due to drinking, partying with different men and had a big craving for cocaine.

"Clarissa was arrested for drug possession, child neglect and resisting arrest.

CPS took your daughter and she's been gone for a couple weeks now. I had no way of contacting you until now."

Uncle Elroy stood in his doorway smoking a cigarette as he continued to tell Frankie the news about his daughter with his robe wide open. "She's gone Frankie, she's gone far away and you may never get to see her again." Elroy shouted with smoke exiting from his nostrils.

"Well do you know where I can go to try and get her back?" Frankie asked with a concerned look on his face.

Elroy hollered "Listen Frankie, Clarissa done fucked up and got that child taken away from her. She's been fucking up for the past 10 years. You didn't do no better out here in these streets slanging and dealing drugs. Both of you partying and fighting like cats and dogs, no wonder that child is in the system."

"Listen here!" Elroy shouted puffing on his cigarette. "I will make a few calls to see what I can do to get you some information about my niece. Now if you want to see your baby girl again Frankie, I suggest you head over to child protective services and cop a plea with their asses because I've washed my hands clean of this shit. I'm done." Elroy screamed, slamming the door in Frankie's face destroying every ounce of hope he had that day. Frankie's pride was dropped down to his lowest point and drinking became one of his biggest habits.

Life was gloomy for quite some time until he met Lady and fell head over hills. To Frankie's surprise, Lady had just ended a rocky relationship of her own. Lady agreed to date Frankie after they talked for hours one sunny afternoon. Frankie treated Lady with respect, like a gentleman. He took her out to the Whispers concert, where they danced their hearts out, and then treated her to dinner at a fine Italian restaurant in New York City. After a few dates, Frankie made plans to come pick Lady up and take her to meet his family.

Frankie knew from the first time he laid eyes on Lady that she was going to be his wife. Frankie drove across town over to the South Side of Jamaica Queens to pick his lady up. When he arrived, there Lady stood smiling at him carrying a four-month old bundle of joy. Without a second thought, Frankie skidded over to the curb, jumped out of his car, and ran around to place his new love and her beautiful baby girl inside. Then the three of them headed over to his mother's house across town. "How you feeling today Lady?" Frankie asked his new girl as they drove away.

"Oh, I'm doing just fine, glad to be with you again." Lady answered smiling at Frankie. "Me too Lady, you look beautiful by the way and you smell good as hell, damn." Lady laughed as Frankie made noises cursing about how beautiful she looked. She found him to be very funny and handsome as well. "Thank you, Frankie," Lady smiled while kissing Frankie on his cheek. Receiving a kiss from Lady set Frankie's soul on fire.

When Frankie arrived at his mother's house, he immediately set up a comfort zone for Lady and her new baby. He then ran out of the living room, around the corner to the kitchen so he could fix them both two grilled cheese sandwiches with iced cold glasses of Coca- Cola.

Everyone, from Frankie's grandmother, to his mother, down to his four brothers and sisters, all fussed with each other about who was taking the longest holding the baby. Lady was pleased and very happy because she felt right at home with Frankie's family. As Frankie washed the dishes, he watched the bread in the frying pan so that it wouldn't burn on each side before he filled the bread with cheese.

Entering the kitchen, Frankie's mother noticed her son crying at the sink. Frankie cried because he was happy. He was also deeply saddened to know that he couldn't see his firstborn child. When Frankie's mother walked over to her son, she rubbed his back softly saying, "Don't cry Frankie, don't cry. You are truly blessed, my son. God has sent you a beautiful baby girl and she is sitting right out there in my living room. Love her with all your heart, you hear," Frankie's mother cried softly, with tears rolling down her cheeks and over her red lipstick.

Frankie just shook his head in agreement with his mother as he hugged her. After that Frankie and Lady were inseparable.

*   *   *   *   *   *

"Now your grandmother, my mother, was a dancer. One of the most beautiful dancers out!" Frankie spoke while smiling in the kitchen. "Gram' was a child of 8 children and back in her day, they were very poor at one point. As teens, her and her sisters saw great opportunities and they grabbed them quick. They went out into the world and made shit happen. Catching gigs dancing at the Cotton club and The Flamingo." Frankie continued. "When I was a youngster, me and my siblings would watch our mother before each show as she stepped out with amazement."

"They had the most beautiful costumes I had ever seen filled with diamond studs, leather and lace. They wore furs in every color. They were fly as fuck! Frankie shouted joking with his daughters. Several years had passed and Lady had two girls by Frankie along with her oldest daughter Kai' making three children all together. As their girls sat at the kitchen table in their apartment in Jamaica Queens. Frankie shouted "Now I'm not talking about these broads in our era who be dancing up in these clubs where they forgot to get dressed, buck naked and high as a kite."

Frankie's daughters died laughing looking over at their mother while she cooked breakfast smiling to herself. Frankie grinned.

"No not my fucking mother! Your grandmother had class. She danced around rich *fellas* like Sinatra and his pack!"

"The Ladies who danced!" Frankie shouted smiling from ear- to- ear. Frankie would go on and on about how proud he was of his beautiful mother and aunts. Every morning, his daughters would get an earful before they were led off to school.

Lady noticed a slight change in her husband's behavior but was scared to confront him about it. As her kids filled their bags with books and readied themselves for school, Lady stood in the dark hallway near the kitchen knocking on the bathroom door. Then she waited patiently for a response.

Frankie shouted, "Yeah baby, I'll be out in a minute." On the other side of the door was the sound of running water and the toilet flushing two times or more while Frankie was inside snorting hits of coke. As the door flew open, Frankie walked out of the bathroom to see his wife standing there. "What's the matter baby? Why you standing there like that? Are you alright?" Frankie asked his wife, softly placing his hand on her cheek and then through her hair.

Lady answered "Yes I'm fine Frank. But you know the rent was due five days ago and I asked you over a week ago about this."

"So, what's going on? Why you looking at me like you seen a ghost or something?" Frankie started ranting and raving and pacing back and forth throughout the apartment like a madman. He then walked to the back towards their bedroom. He opened the closet and kneeled on one knee on the floor by his safe.

14

Frankie mumbled underneath his breath as he remembered the numbers to the combination. Then he opened the safe, pulled out a wad of cash and headed back towards the front to the living room. When Frankie reached the front of the apartment, his eyes became wide and full of surprise to see his wife sitting there laughing and giggling on the phone with her sister Roxi. Lady saw Frankie standing there but continued with her conversation.

Frankie hinted "Lady why don't you call her back I need to talk to you. Lady replied "Give me a minute baby," signaling him with her fingers. Lady then mentioned "I have to ask Roxi if she could watch the kids for me after school because I have a few errands to run." Covering the phone with her palm saying, "It's important one- minute baby," returning to her conversation still giggling. "So, what we just finished talking about wasn't important huh?" Frankie snarled annoyed at his wife who was ignoring him. Suddenly, Frankie walked over towards Lady saying, "Get the fuck from off the phone." Smacking the phone out of Lady's hand causing her to fall onto the couch.

Lady got up in a split second, jumping onto Frankie's back digging her nails into his head trying to scratch his brains out. Frankie started screaming shouting, "Woman get the fuck off me!" Moving around in circles trying to free himself from Lady's rage.

He then threw the phone across the room saying, "When I say something, I mean it". Repeating his words for the second time. Frankie's eyes were wide open still shocked from his wife's reaction jumping on his back and scratching him on his forehead.

15

Frankie stormed through the living room throwing money onto the couch, with several bills falling to the floor as he exited the apartment without saying another word.

Lady was left sitting on the couch with tears flowing from her eyes. There were several hundred dollar bills spread on top of Lady, the couch and all over the floor.

Lady didn't care at all about the money at this point. She was bothered staring at the door worried about her husband. Thinking that he was no longer the man that she once married. When her oldest daughter Kai walked over to her, while her younger sisters followed and whispered "Don't cry Mommy, everything will be okay." Lady then wiped her tears, placed lunches in each of her daughter's bags, then drove her girls to school.

Frankie worked two jobs during the week. He worked double shifts because he needed a cover for the drug money to keep the police from off his tail. At his first job, he was an electrical engineer for a top-notch construction company. Frankie was in charge of the wiring of different units in buildings being built throughout the city. He also worked part-time at Creedmoor Hospital on Thursday and Friday as a security guard. A job that he got from his mom who worked as a nurse for over 20 years. Since it was Friday, Frankie stood at his post calmly waiting for his shift to end.

As the time slowly approached for him to clock out, he went up to every floor in the building and made his rounds for the day. When Frankie left the hospital, his pager went off. Frankie sighed to himself because he could hardly read his pager and run at the same time.

He was running trying to get from out of the pouring rain. Before Frankie entered his car, he decided to run across the street over to the deli to call the number that was left on his pager. "Hello," Frankie greeted.

"What's happening my man? Did you get off your shift? I have a few things I need you to carry over to Jersey, so how soon could you make it uptown?" Frankie's uncle asked, waiting anxiously for an answer. "Hey Frankie, you gotta give me a time now I got these people waiting on me now!"

"Ok Unc, I'll be there shortly. If I leave now, I'll beat rush hour and it will take me at least thirty minutes to get uptown," Frankie replied.

"Ok see you then." Bobby answered hanging up the phone.

Frankie's days were filled with hours of hard work. But his nights, belonged to the streets! First stop was Murty's Bar and Grill over on 114th street, up in Harlem. Frankie ran over to his car, ducking the rain drops.

As he gave his car time to warm up, he thought to himself real hard about his wife and how he's been acting lately. He wanted to call her and tell her how sorry he was for treating her the way he did, but couldn't find the courage to do so. He began to think of all the things she liked and what he could do to make things right again with him and his Lady. Frankie rolled through traffic onto the Triborough, across the bridge with music blasting in his tan Cadillac Deville. Singing along with the sweet melodies of the Whispers playing on the radio, shouting, "I love you, oh I love you, said I love you Lady..." Thinking of his Lady's face.

The louder he sang, the harder he thought. The harder he thought, the faster he drove.

Zipping through the Eastside of Harlem, catching every green light, he arrived at the bar in exactly thirty minutes. "What's up Uncle Murt?" Frankie shouted across the floor to where his uncle sat. Murt gave him a nod, raising his glass of Cognac along with a friendly smile. His uncle Bobby had already walked over to him explaining a few things he needed his nephew to make happen for the night. Bobby and Murt had their hands into every aspect of the business that you could think of. They owned a business called Spotless Cleaners, where the cleaning company cleaned up any and all blood stains due to bloody gunshot and stab wounds. These guys cleaned up like professionals, leaving clothes, houses, cars and crime scenes spotless. Their business expanded quickly. And The payments they received to clean up were incredible. Running this kind of business was dangerous. They were very careful and always alert. There were plenty accidents, murders and dangerous people who placed orders daily.

Bobby and Murt were cold-blooded loan sharks who were knee-deep into the drug game. They cut no slack to anyone who owed them bread. The community love the two brothers for giving all the kids in the neighborhood jobs in the many stores they owned. Loyalty and respect was real and one hand washed the other. Frankie would bartend some nights at Murty's Bar. Every now and then, his uncles would throw extravagant white and black affairs where Frankie would perform. Frankie played the saxophone like no other!

When he blew his horn, each melody just made love to your eardrums. Frankie pulled endless crowds who would come from all over town to hear him play.

"Hey Frankie come over here!" Murt shouted, as Frankie stood talking to Bobby in private behind the bar. Bobby had placed a small white piece of paper into Frankie's hand with a list of names and addresses of about five different people he put a hit on. Frankie was his uncle's personal hit man when necessary. And It looked like tonight was one of those nights. Frankie stopped the conversation he was having with his uncle Bobby and asked about the man who was sitting with his uncle Murt. Instead of answering, Bobby signaled his nephew as they both walked across the floor to the seating area.

As Frankie walked across the floor, he sized up the funny looking short fellah who looked upset and leery about his ways. When Frankie reached his uncle Murt, Murt smacked Frankie lightly across the cheek while he kissed the other saying, "Frankie meet Yancy. Yancy, this is my nephew Frankie." Murt continued "Now the two of you will be doing some work together."

The two men shook hands, looking each other up and down, checking one another out. 'Yeah! Yancy's father did business with us for more than twenty years bless his soul," Murt mentioned shaking his head as he switched his toothpick from side to side, finally laying it to the right side of his mouth. Murt shook his glass of cognac slowly thinking to himself, *That piece of shit had it coming for a long time.'*

Knowing that Yancy's father was one of the many names his brother Bobby placed into Frankie's hand for him to hit, Murt sipped his cognac slowly as he gazed into his nephew's eyes with the look of disgust when he spoke of Yancy's father, 'Pops. Pops, moved several kilos of coke and dope from state to state with Bobby and Murt when they were young in the game.

He had also witnessed numerous murders and endless piles of money throughout the years of doing business together. Unfortunately, Yancy's father came up on rough times and needed to borrow more than he could handle. Pops borrowed over $90,000 from the brothers. He was given more than a five- year span to pay it back, due their personal friendship. During that time, Pops paid a measly $5000 of it back and that was a problem.

Every day that passed, Pops just blew shit off like everything was gravy. Until one day he was found dead with a bullet in his head, shot between the eyes execution style. Pops owed entirely too much money. So, this murder was a no-brainer for the two brothers. Hiring Yancy was a smart business move. As many would say, keep your friends close and your enemies closer.

Although Yancy had absolutely no idea of the events involving the three in the connection to his father's murder, he still seemed very leery and unfocused. His situation was understandable but very strange. "I really don't want to work with this motherfucker." Frankie thought to himself still staring at Yancy. "Yeah, I want you to show Yancy the ropes around here Frankie. Put him on to the good life," Bobby said, moving his hands with each gesture.

Frankie and Yancy were now partners in crime trafficking huge quantities of drugs from state to state.

*   *   *   *   *   *

"Huhhh." The loud sound roared from Frankie's bedroom as he screamed at the top of his lungs. Lady was sleeping next to her husband and jumped up saying "Omg Frankie! Are you ok?" Lady then grabbed a cloth when she realized Frankie was in a deep sleep and started wiping his head that was dripping with sweat. Lady tried to wake Frankie who was having a bad dream. "It was just a bad dream Frank." Lady responded moving the cloth downward to his chest. Frankie didn't answer her, still stuck in a deep sleep.

"Moving rapidly wiping off any evidence and fingerprints that may be found at one of the apartments of his victim. Who lay slumped over in a chair with his throat slashed from ear- to- ear in a pool of his own blood." "Frankie was very careful when he was out on a hit. He killed each victim differently so that the murders never led back to him. Frankie recaptures one of his murders in his dream sliding out of a bedroom window, down the side of the building from a cable wire strapped to his body to escape after killing his victim with his uncle Murt waiting anxiously in his Mercedes wagon. The loud sounds of the sirens in his dream woke him up out of his sleep."

When Frankie woke up, he jumped out of the bed looking at the clock realizing that it was ten minutes passed six. Then he quickly showered and dressed.

Frankie had a few kilos to move out of town with Yancy tonight and he couldn't be late. Although Frankie hadn't been feeling well, he was happy to sleep through the day with his wife in his arms until he had another one of those bad dreams that seemed to surface practically every other night since his first murder.

Frankie pulled up to the bar with his music blasting in his ride. His windows were closed but you could still hear the tunes from inside.

As Frankie opened his door, Yancy made his way over dancing to the beat, sweating like a pig in heat. Frankie shouted, "I see you," smiling at Yancy as he continued dancing, with sweat stains visible through the armpits of his shirt. Frankie laughed as he entered the bar with a rack of suits fresh from the cleaners. "Hey Frankie," Jacklyn purred, sitting at the bar with one of her good friends.

Frankie looked at Jacklyn and replied "How you doing baby." Walking through the bar to the back and up the stairs to his uncle's office, Frankie knocked on Murt's door and waited patiently for an answer.

Murt screamed, "Who the fuck is it?"

Frankie quickly answered, 'It's me Unc. It's Frankie."

Talking to one of his female concubines, Murt whispered "Let him in, will you?" When Frankie stepped into the room, Murt was occupied with one of his sweethearts for the day. There was a huge bottle of Jack Daniels and visible lines of powder on the table.

Murt and his woman continued playing blackjack as Frankie strolled past them and into the next room.

Deciding that he needed to change, he pulled a suit out of the closet. Frankie stepped back into the room his uncle was in wearing a custom-tailored beige suit with some dark brown gators. His shirt matched his shoes and was slightly open, enough so that his diamond studded chains could show. Murt shouted "Ooo Whee!" Would you look at those threads? "You stepping out today nephew!"

Frankie smiled and shouted "You know it," as he headed over to the small antique tables and chairs in the corner. He pulled out a small pocket mirror and poured coke over top of it. Frankie sniffed and drank a few shots of his uncle's Jack Daniels, getting his mind right for the night.

"You make sure to really be careful out there on them roads, you hear?! And make sure that motherfucker down stairs is paying attention. You gotta watch his ass, because I can smell him sweating from up here."

Frankie laughed saying "Ok Unc!" As he cleaned up shop, Frankie went into the bathroom to rinse his hands. He looked into the mirror making sure there was no powder residue on his nose. As he cleaned his face, Frankie started coughing up blood and couldn't understand why. He coughed in the bathroom uncontrollably for two minutes cleaned himself up and made his way back down stairs to the bar. As Frankie walked across the room Jacklyn smiled at him, trying to make eye contact while she stirred at her drink with a straw.

She was wearing a short red mink stole that wrapped around her skin tight black mini dress with matching stiletto heels. When Frankie reached the door, Jacklyn said "I'll be waiting here for you when you get back Frankie," giggling with her girlfriend.

Frankie turned around, looked at her and her friend and blurted "Not tonight Jack," slamming the door behind him. The bartender working the bar that evening, burst out laughing. Jacklyn's girlfriend Lilly laughed as well, until she shut up from the stares of her angry friend.

Jacklyn had it bad for Frankie and she tried numerous times to get him into her bed. The same bed where she had lay down with many men, baring six children with a different dad for each one. No matter how good she looked or how hard she tried, he shut her down at every try. Pulling herself together after the door slammed, she focused on forgetting about Frankie and readying herself for the next Kat who walked through.

As Frankie stepped outside, he noticed his uncle transferring bricks from the back of Yancy's truck into his Deville. Yancy just sat inside of his truck shaking like a leaf.

Yancy had been a hardcore dope fiend for years, until he decided to clean up and go to rehab. He had stayed clean for months, but then the death of his father hit him hard, straight to the chest. Yancy started using again. He would take a little bit of the drugs from each brick of dope they bagged, after each count and before each drop.

Yancy needed a fix tonight as he looked through the rear-view mirror at Bobby and Frankie hoping they wouldn't notice he was high sweating like he was standing in a thunderstorm with no umbrella.

Yancy sat in his truck wiping all the sweat from off his face and forehead. The little pieces of tissue he had didn't help him at all. They were all broken up into little wet pieces. He quickly threw the tissue into the ashtray and began wiping his face with his shirt. Bobby was just finishing packing. He closed Yancy's truck, carrying a big duffel bag upstairs and placing it into his safe. Then he locked up everything and returned down to the front of the bar so he could further discuss some business with his nephew. Bobby explained each detail carefully, giving Frankie descriptions of the Bosses he would meet. He also explained the different towns and gave brief instructions of the distance, including tolls and every other necessary detail he could think of.

"Be careful out there nephew, and call me soon as you reach your destination," Bobby said, as he hugged his nephew.

"I gotcha Unc," Frankie replied. Everything will be smooth, like butter baby!" "Hey Bobby, let me ask you one thing before I go." Frankie pondered with a look of concern on his face.

Bobby looked at Frankie and said "Well don't hold back now, what's up?"

"Well I've been thinking about this for a while now and I wondered what you thought about me buying Lady a brand-new Benz," Frankie whispered lightly.

Bobby screamed "Mercedes?!" "Damn Frankie what the fuck did you do this time? Shit! I give it to Lady, because she surely knows how to put up with your shit and you sure know how to give it to her. But when it's time to make up my man, you make shit up." Bobby moved his feet from side to side, laughing in his nephew's face. "Lady deserves it all." Bobby shouted, hugging his nephew and wishing him a safe trip back.

Frankie had to think long and hard about the decisions he needed to make concerning his family's security and future. Frankie found out he was dying of a disease that hit the streets hard in the early 80's. He was in denial and caught a wakeup call when he coughed up blood in the restroom. He's been feeling sick for weeks with flu like symptoms and hot flashes. He just brushed it off thinking he had a cold. He had no idea what was wrong with him. Frankie was a very healthy man. He never cheated on his wife and he had a physical at his doctor's office every year. One day Frankie made an appointment to go and get himself checked out. Frankie thought to himself as he remembered his visit to the doctor. "Frankie, you have a disease called HIV. The virus that causes AIDS. This disease attacks the immune system and reduces the number of T-cells in the body that helps fight off infections and harmful bacteria. AIDS can be contracted through sexual activity, through the transfer of body fluids and through drug use by sharing needles. Frankie, you have less than six months to live. Here's a list of therapists that you can call as well as my direct number, you need to get these prescriptions filled out immediately. So, sorry to inform you of this terrible news Frankie." The doctor delivered the worst news ever. Frankie couldn't believe it. This disease is fatal and it wiped out millions of people in the Black and Latino community instantly.

Frankie thought about what the doctor told him and he knew exactly how he caught the disease. Frankie made a fatal mistake when he tried dope for the first time, sharing an infected needle with Yancy. Yancy's been carrying the disease for several months and he knew he was infected, but never told a soul. Frankie was heartbroken to know he was dying and couldn't do a damn thing about it. He had gotten so caught up in the street life, that it swallowed him up and took over his whole world. A few years ago, when Frankie worked construction, he had a terrible accident, falling off the scaffolding on a site at a building he was working on breaking his leg and fracturing his ribs. Frankie was under a tremendous amount of pain, even after surgery, which led him to start using pain killers and prescribed barbiturates. He had gotten addicted to the pills and started abusing them. After a while, Frankie's body became immune to pain killers, forcing him to seek something much stronger to ease his pain. Frankie partied, drank booze and dabbled with drugs here and there but who didn't? He challenged many sins and devils on different levels just like any other man. In his lifetime, Frankie has painted the most beautiful pictures by hand, played the most beautiful melodies and married the most beautiful woman of his dreams.

It was their Era! The signs of the times. Frankie lived life well and did it his way. Living the lavish life had its dark side that quickly came to an end. He was adored by many especially his children. The greatest people in your life are always the first to leave you. In Frankie's children's eyes, he was their dad who did no wrong. Frankie's immune system was getting weaker and he lost a tremendous amount of weight. The handsome tall man that once walked this earth was deteriorating and returning to dust.

27

HOOD GAMES

Frankie knew he was dying and had to come clean and face the love of his life. After avoiding it for months, Frankie picked Lady up one evening to share the seriousness of his condition. He drove with his wife to their special place out on the beach to deliver the worse news of his life. "Lady my love I am so afraid. I don't know how to tell you this." Frankie whispered looking at the waves in the water. "Tell me what Frankie? What's going on?" Lady asked turning Frankie's face towards hers staring into her husband's eyes. Frankie answered Lady with tears in his eyes saying "I am dying and I'm giving you my will, my money and the keys to this new Benz. I've been using Heroin and caught a fatal disease that cannot be cured. Please forgive me baby. I can't even face you right now. Why Me? I'm so confused." Frankie cried on the beach pouring his heart out to his wife. Lady just hugged Frankie as he cried on her shoulder. She cried with him scared to death of the news her husband just revealed. Lady didn't know what to do. The only thing she could do at that moment was be strong for her husband and their three children. The shock of having such a rare and fatal disease was more than a burden on Frankie's soul. He felt that there was no use in crying over spilled milk. The ship had already sailed and the only thing he wanted more than anything in the world was to take care of his family.

Things took a turn for the worse. Yancy started stealing everything he could get his wet hands on. Large quantities of dope started missing from every delivery they brought out of town making Frankie and his uncles look bad. Yancy started looking utterly suspicious whenever they drove in and out of state, unable to control the water that poured out of his face making himself look guilty. It finally came to the point of no return.

Frankie sent Yancy off to see his Pops six feet under. Everything was falling apart. And something had to give quick. Bobby and Murt decided to take a break from the drug game for a while. They made a few calls and set up a huge drug deal in Miami with their friend Hector which was a huge success for the two brothers. Frankie's uncle's retired after selling their friend Hector and his cousin Vinnie a large quantity of cocaine and took a long vacation in Costa Rica where they made the best of having lots of money and their freedom.

After killing Yancy, Frankie passed away a few months later and the rain just wouldn't stop falling. Frankie's uncles were devastated to lose their nephew so suddenly. They made sure all his funeral arrangements expenses and family were taken care of. Lady's eyes cried so much that even when they were closed the tears overflowed leaking over her lashes. Her apartment became her safe haven. She didn't want to see or speak to anyone for weeks. Until one sunny day, when she crawled out of her bed and looked at her beautiful brown face in the mirror and smiled. She then told herself *"I will not be broken like my heart."* Lady went out and partied like it was 1999.

*   *   *   *   *   *

HOOD GAMES

"There were so many times when you would cross my mind and then I'd cry a little harder. Just thinking of the days of many times and ways that I said I miss you father. So many nights I would cry and when I tossed and turned I'd say why even bother. It's just the sound of his voice or that picture in the frame just thinking of my father. There are so many children in this world that have holes in their hearts because they lack love from the man who may have left too soon or they've never met."

"Many men today would rather pick up a gun and kill their own brother instead picking up their own son. Don't get me wrong now, because there are still a few good apples up in that tree of life. Who choose to love their kids whether they're with the mother or not! For all you men out there who need a definition of what hard is, let me tell you that being hard is sitting down at the dinner table cracking jokes with your kids.

"Being gangster is sharing and caring. Even if you only have a penny to your name, it wouldn't matter because you're there to wash away the pain and that's priceless."

"Being street is showing your children how to read and write and the difference between right and wrong, even if you're never right, and filling their minds with knowledge of self and wisdom and their hearts with courage. The first teachers all children meet in their lives are their parents. So please give your seed you planted with love a chance to grow. "All and all if you're here or if you're square; we still need you father."

BREAKING MY WORLD

CHAPTER
Two

"Hey Mona, where you going? Why you always running from me huh? Stop acting like that! Come here!" Waynie whispered, with a low but serious sounding voice as he grabbed his cousin's hand."

Mona's mother Lady had a hectic schedule, working a full-time job with double shifts. It was a whole new ball game after Frankie died and shit was real in the field. Lady had to face her fears, juggling three kids with no husband around to hold her down. She worked the graveyard shift five nights a week over at the hospital. Tonight, she was in desperate need of a sitter since the one she hired had called and cancelled at the last minute.

"I can't be late for work another shift or I'll be in trouble," Lady thought to herself as she showered before getting dressed for her shift at work. "Come over here girls." Lady called her three girls to her bedroom to explain a few things to them before heading off to work. "Mommy has to go to work tonight, ok? Kai, make sure to look after your sisters. I will have one of your cousins come up to check on you while I'm gone." Lady prepared her daughters for the night while she put on her lipstick and looked into the mirror. Lady's girls weren't babies at all, they understood exactly what their mother told them and followed her instructions.

Whenever the sitter Lady hired was unavailable, she had a family member check on her daughters so there would be no worries while she worked.

Lady ran to the supermarket before she headed to work. She picked up a few snacks for her kids and brought some turkey wings, onions and rice so she could prep and cook for dinner when she got off. On her way, back from the store, Lady saw her nephew Waynie, sitting with his boys in the projects. "Hi Waynie," Lady greeted her nephew with a smile before she gave him a hug.

"Hi Aunt Lady," Waynie answered sliding his beer up under the bench so his aunt wouldn't see it.

"Listen Waynie, I need a quick favor. Could you check on the girls in about an hour or two? I have to be at work like right now and the babysitter cancelled at the last minute." Lady looked at Waynie with a stern look on her face, waiting for an answer.

"Sure, Aunt Lady, I can do that, no problem," Waynie answered as he sat back on the bench with his friends. Waynie agreed and set Lady's mind at ease.

She hurried back to her apartment, dropped off the groceries and headed off to work for the night. She also gave him a few dollars for his troubles. Lady was in panic mode because she was already running behind schedule.

Waynie didn't have shit else to do but drink and talk shit with his boys anyway. It was Friday night and the premiere movie "The Exorcist" was showing on television in an hour.

Kai was upstairs cooking a new brand sausage called knockwurst. The sausages were huge and they tasted just like franks.

Lady had taught her oldest daughter how to cook a few easy meals that she could prepare when she wasn't at home with them. Kai had learned to cook simple shit like mac and cheese, microwaveable foods, franks and beans and grilled cheese sandwiches, which was their father's favorite. Their house was always blessed with plenty of food. They never went hungry due to those food stamp books in different colors depending on how much money you had. The brown books were $1 and the purple books were $5. It was crazy ripping those joints out at the grocery store.

Kai always took her sisters to the store with her when it was time to go food shopping. Once they got there, she'd send Mona inside with the food stamp books and a long list of items they needed for the house. Mona would be highly upset standing at the register with the stamps. It looked and felt like Monopoly money. Lady's girls hated when that time of the month came up, when the three of them had to stand outside with their mother on that long ass line with what looked to be like a million people, waiting for hours to get one huge block of cheese.

That cheese was good as all hell though, once you could cut that shit. The cheese was so thick that you damn near broke the knife trying to cut a piece. But it was worth the struggle tell you that much. Kai's sister Mona was still at the kitchen table, finishing her homework with an attitude, annoyed at each question.

Kai had been given specific orders from her mother to make sure that both her sisters finished all their work from school before any play. Mona wasn't happy at all and couldn't wait to get up from that table.

Mona sucked her teeth because her younger sister Mia was already finished. "Mia, come in here and help me make some Kool-Aid, okay?" Kai shouted as she washed out the pitcher in the sink.

"Okay," Mia replied as she ran from the living room into the kitchen. Mona looked at her sisters and rolled her eyes. Kai peeped Mona hating because Mia was free from homework, so she started laughing at her sister to fuck with her nerves.

"You didn't finish that shit yet?" Kai asked Mona, smiling while opening the packet of Kool-Aid. "Damn! I see you might be having a long night over there at that table," Kai giggled staring at Mona. Mona ignored her sister, filling out each math question without caring what it said. Mona couldn't take it any longer, plus her thinking cap been shut off a long time ago.

Kai placed a wooden stool in the kitchen for Mia to stand on, since she was too short to reach the counter. Mia slowly made her way onto the stool. As she began to climb, Mona asked "Can I help?" Kai then signaled Mona to come over and told her to get two lemons out of the fridge and some ice cubes from the freezer.

Mona got the lemons and placed them onto the counter. When she went to get the ice cubes from the freezer, she heard a knock at the door and went to go answer it.

Jumping up at the peep hole, Mona noticed that it was Waynie as she screamed his name to Kai before opening the door.

Waynie entered the apartment and Mona was already running back to the kitchen. Waynie grabbed her hand, asking her all types of questions. *'Hey Mona, where you going? Why you always running from me huh? Stop acting like that! Come here!'* Mona wasn't thinking about anything that Waynie just said because she had lemons to cut. Waynie went and sat in the living room to watch television, flipping through the channels until he stopped at the basketball game.

Kai shouted "We are getting ready to watch *'The Exorcist* in a little while Waynie. The premiere is coming on tonight."

Still watching the game, Waynie answered

"Okay." Kai rolled her eyes looking at her sisters as they all made faces at him. While Mona cut the lemons into slices, she watched her sister struggling with the spoon because her hands were too little to stir. Mona burst out laughing because Mia's body was moving weirdly as she stirred, grunting with each movement. The more she stirred, the louder she grunted; splashing Kool-Aid all over the counter and floor.

Kai and Mona were dying laughing because she just couldn't get a grip of that spoon for nothing. Mia laughed too, thinking she was doing a great job. They were all having a great time until Waynie interrupted and said "What's so funny?" breaking the girl's laughter as he opened the freezer to place two forty ounces of beer inside. When Waynie opened the freezer, the girls continued to laugh silently.

Giggling because he couldn't see their heads while the freezer door was open. After Kai was finally able to catch her breath from laughing, she went and got some paper towels then asked Mona to help her wipe up the mess that Mia made. The girls all looked very nice that day because their mother had treated them to getting their hair washed and set along with her when she picked them up from school.

Mona and Mia's hair was done up in a ponytail with their hair out in the back with long bangs. Kai liked to wear her hair braids, so she got her hair done in two long cornrows. Their mother wore her hair out, with it flowing down her back, and had the front cut in short bangs. Lady brought her daughters two nice outfits a piece with shoes to match because their behavior had been extremely well lately.

Which didn't make a bit of difference because they were spoiled by her good or not! Kai's mom called the house to check up on her and the girls and asked her to run out to the store because she forgot to buy lunch meat for the week. Kai didn't want to go, but she knew her mother would be highly upset if she didn't have any sandwiches to make for lunch the next day.

Kai decided to go to the store before the movie started. She went in the kitchen and turned all the switches to the stove off and placed the lids on all the pots. "Mona, make sure that Mia stays away from the oven until I get back from the store." Kai said pointing to the kitchen. There was still about 20 minutes until the movie started, so Kai had enough time to get to the store and back. Kai gave Mia half of her knockwurst on her way out the door.

Their mother made an exception that night to let them eat in the living room while they watched the movie as long as they didn't make a mess.

They had a big screen television in their living room, with a beautiful couch set and entertainment system that their mother didn't want fucked up, scratched or stained at all. Stepping into her shell tops, Kai yelled "I'll be right back y'all," promising Mia and Mona some candy and a quarter juice when she returned. Waynie then called out to Kai, before the door closed, asking her to get him some French fries from the Chinese restaurant and whatever she wanted. After locking the door, Waynie went back into the kitchen where he sat placing his weed into a Philly.

Mona went to the back to get some blankets and pillows so she and her sisters could lay out on the carpet once the movie started. Waynie was watching every move Mona made, looking at her in ways that he shouldn't. Puffing on his blunt admiring her little curves. When Mona came back, she laid on the floor and then realized that she had to pee so she got back up and made her way towards the bathroom.

Waynie asked, "Where you going Mona?"

"To the bathroom," Mona answered, running passed the kitchen to the bathroom closing the door. After using the restroom, Mona began washing her hands singing to herself looking in the mirror when she heard a knock at the door. Mona's little sister Mia's eyes were glued to the television, with food in front of her so there was no reason for her to step out of her space.

"Who is it?" Mona asked, staring at the door while wiping her hands with some tissue. There was no answer. All of a sudden the door opened and the lights went out with her and Waynie inside.

"Why you been ignoring me, huh?" Waynie snarled angrily, as he reached out and grabbed Mona . Mona didn't respond. Waynie lifted up her skirt yanking Mona's little body frontward towards the toilet placing his rough crusty fingers into her panties. Waynie felt Mona's vagina as she tried to stop him from touching her. He struggled with Mona while feeling on her vagina. Waynie was having his way with her as she cried quietly. Then he took his hands out of her panties and turned her around quickly forcing his penis into her mouth saying, "I saw the way you were looking at me today, teasing me with that little ass skirt you're wearing."

Going deeper into her mouth, pulling her hair as tight as he could. Mona cried to herself with tears running over his crusty black penis. Waynie was making noises like he was making love to his woman and then he finally slowed down. Waynie quickly released himself from Mona throwing her to the floor. He then grabbed a washcloth, wet it and started wiping himself. After cleaning himself, he picked Mona up from the floor wiping her tears saying "If you tell anybody about what just happened, I'll fucking kill you – you hear me?" Pointing his finger into Mona's forehead. Mona shook her head up and down.

Mona was scared to death and didn't know what to do. Both Waynie and Mona exited the bathroom. He then went to the freezer and poured himself a tall glass of beer so he could watch the movie with his cousins.

When Kai got back from the store, the movie had already started. Kai was glad to see that Mona didn't eat yet. She thought that her sister waited for her to return from the store. When Kai sat down on the floor with Mia, she looked up and saw that Mona was already crying.

"Stop being a big baby Mona, it's only a movie," Kai mentioned as she smiled at her sister, knowing that Mona hated scary movies but would watch them if everyone watched along with her. Mona was afraid of scary movies, but "The Exorcist" was the scariest movie she had ever seen...

MONA

CHAPTER
Three

Where did I go wrong? Mona asked? "It wasn't supposed to be this way." The young girl mumbled underneath the pain of flowing tears. Lying helplessly in a fetal position collecting on all the thoughts of yesterday. Her eyes bloodshot red from crying. Staring up at the only two people who shared her pain, her sisters Kai and Mia. It was just the three of them against the world. They were all so close, always looking out for one another, wiping each other's tears keeping one another strong.

There were so many unanswered questions and thoughts racing through Mona's head. Mona's dad had passed away when she was only seven years old. Just when she was getting to know him, bam, he was gone forever. Even though he was gone physically, the bond between them stayed in her heart mentally connected for all eternity. Mona loved her father so much. She really wished he was here for her now.

So sad and hurt by the loss of her father. The young girl witnessed her dad at his funeral shocked and confused; Mona just smiled so her family couldn't see her pain. She was the middle child of three girls. Slim with long brown hair wearing two ponytails and long bangs that covered the puffiness of her beautiful light brown eyes which complimented her light skinned complexion.

There was something about Mona, she had that fire in her eyes. No one could quite pinpoint what that fire was, but everyone sure was in for a rude awakening.

Although Mona thought she was in control, Kai always stepped on her toes to let her know who was running shit. The girls lived in a two-bedroom apartment with their mother Lady. Mia and Mona looked up to Kai because she was basically all they knew when their mother wasn't around. Mommy had started going out more with her new friends, to ease the pain of Daddy being gone. When Daddy died, it hurt like hell! A lot of confusion and loneliness filled Mona's little heart since she was so young at the time of his death.

"I look just like him." Mona thought, looking in the mirror noticing her resemblance. She wondered and worried if her mother was strong enough to raise three young girls on her own. Children bear witness to more than you know. The eyes of a child see much farther than their mouths can tell.

Once a child comes of age, his/her need to react is like clockwork. Everything happens in due season and all acts manifests in its own settings. Mona held in quite a lot and had experienced far too much at a young age. This molded her into a wise young girl, building an inner strength that no one could ever touch. Being a young girl, experiencing her father's death and then facing molestation by someone she trusted and knew; was a very painful, traumatic ordeal.

Mona went through a stage in her life that was very hard for her. She fell into a deep depression and sadness. Feeling like everything that happened to her was her fault.

HOOD GAMES

Children who witness or experience abuse sexually, physically or mentally become very vulnerable and have nowhere to turn when they are over powdered by their abuser. Things like this happen on a daily basis and so many children become victims of sexual abuse at an early age.

"If you ever become a victim of abuse in any way never be afraid to tell a family member or public authority. It is never your fault and you have all the rights in the world to be protected and feel safe from all harm."

Mona listened carefully as she watched the television show, discussing sexual and physical abuse in the home. Mona stared at the television searching for answers. She was so angry and frustrated not being able to tell anyone what was wrong with her. It silenced her spiritually and damaged her inner soul. Mona was searching for an outlet, and she just wanted to be free from her pain.

Hard times were passing by and Mona was becoming very alert and aware of all activities in and out of their apartment. Mona and her family lived in Baisley Projects! One of the toughest projects in Queens.

Everyone came to the projects. Mad people would hang up and down the hills, in the basketball courts and at the cab stand. The cab stand was a little shack that everyone hung out at called "The Spot."

It was decked with arcade games like Mrs. Pacman and Centipede. There was a dispatcher at the end of the corridor who handled any and all business transactions. All the big-timers stayed at the spot. Some would come in the cab stand to chill, have a drink or two and play a few video games.

While other big timers didn't play any games at all. The cab stand stayed open all night and business was #1 priority! Mona's aunt Roxi lived in a different building from her mom. Roxi's building was directly across the street from the cab stand. She basically had a clear shot to everything that popped off on the corner in the hood. Mona peeped all the action from Roxi's window when she visited her aunt after school.

Whoever knocked on Roxi's door, either played basketball, instruments or had some type of talent. Every kid at Roxi's house was talented. Roxi's kids, all her nieces and nephews and even her grandkids. They were the 'Jacksons of the projects. Roxi's kids had a studio built in their room. The boys played all instruments, made tracks and hot beats, and all the girls sang and danced and wrote their own songs. Roxi was a great role model for all the kids in the hood. Her boys also played basketball very well. She was a basketball mom and she coached for her boys and their friends basketball team. Roxi was a great woman who was very much involved with the community.

BMW's, Mercedes and Jeeps were lined up down the hill every day, one after another, in different colors with a hoe in each ride. Whenever Mona went outside, she tagged behind her sister Kai. That way Kai could keep an eye on her little sister. Things were great in Mona's eyes because everywhere Kai went Mona followed, and the activities got better and better. Each day became an event for everybody. Summer time was lit in the late 80's.

Everybody was outside enjoying themselves waiting for the festivities to begin. Standing down the hill, were a load of chicks in their fly gear.

All the hustlers were out by the basketball court. There was a game that day and all the basketball players showed up to play. Later that evening, would be a jam across the park following the cookout after the big game. Kats were playing ball on the courts, sweating hard trying to impress the girls.

On the scoreboard, the home team was up by twelve points. "*Yes!*" Mona cheered to herself as she sat on the bench with her sister and their Clique. Everybody was smiling and carrying on. Eating lemon cookies and Funyuns from the old man who sold goodies out of his tan frank truck parked on the corner. That frank truck was the bomb! He had all the latest snacks.

"He cooked knishes with the chili stuffed inside, hot sausages and franks. He also sold soda, chips, and all the best candy Lemonheads, Peanut Chews, Red Hots, Chick-o-sticks, and Boston Baked Beans." You name it and he had it!

It was halftime with the home team winning and there were a load of hustlers doing push-ups and pull-ups down the hill by the gate, while other Kats were rolling dice and talking shit. All of a sudden, everything stopped and everyone stared in awe.

As soon as a black BMW pulls up, everybody stood to attention. Stepping out of the car, wearing some spanking white-on-white Nike Cortez, was no other but Vince. Now this man had it all, the Kat was rich with women, good looks, jewels, kids, everything. Vince was fine like wine and he knew it. He also had the kindest heart. He was very generous and would help you out if you were good people.

Vince also had another side to him that was dangerous and vicious. A side that no one wanted to see. Vince played no games when it came to his business and his money. He cut no slack to anyone who dared to cross him.

He knew the streets and that this drug game was nothing to play about. He set the tone with his people and made sure that they clearly understood who was running shit. His motto was "Money, power, respect" and he made sure that he had all three'

Other than that, as long as Vince had it, you had it- simple as that. Vince stayed fresh every day and never wore the same shit twice. He was the first hustler to wear sweatpants with the Le Tigre shorts.. Vince rocked them with a fresh pair of Cortez and had a pair to match every sweat suit. He was the type of person that made you feel good when you saw him. As long as his family was okay, he was a happy man. Vince was tall with a honey brown complexion and wore a low Caesar cut with light brown eyes. His smile was as white as snow and he just glowed in the projects. He was the King! Vince owned the projects and no one would dare to pull his coat too hard or it would be plain murder. Whenever you saw Vince, no matter where it was, his goons followed. He had so many soldiers in the family that people totally lost count.

Every summer would be a display of many events for all the families in the projects. There were basketball and baseball tournaments. The kids had their after-school programs, camps and dance classes down at the community center. Living in the projects was so much fun, it was the place to be.

HOOD GAMES

The hustlers would rent out buses for all the kids to go to Great Adventures with everything paid for, transportation, games, food, and funnel cakes for everybody. Those times were truly the best.

Mona really loved Vince. He had taken a liking to her and her sisters when they really needed someone in their lives since their father was no longer around. Vince just made sure that they were well kept. Some people could never understand the love they all shared for one another, but it is what it is and for some folks, no matter what you do, or how you do it, haters are going hate regardless. The whole Clique stayed laced in every fashion. Mona and her best friend Tony were the youngest out of the bunch. They all grew up together in the projects and it was a hell of a good time. Plenty early morning meetings with Tony at the park as youngsters.

Mona would come to the park with her push pop tops and Tony came with his clay and colorful chalk and they would play skelly with the rest of their friends all day long. All the kids in the projects would battle one another and had different skelly tops, fashionably made with swirls of clay in all different colors. Each building had their own style and team. Playing that game was the best.

Girls would be lined up to play double-dutch in the park while other kids collected soda cans so they all could crush them with their feet and run around the park playing Hot Peas n' Butter and Steal the Bacon.

Late nights all the kids who thought they were grown played Catch and Kiss outside in the park by the barrels.

They shared plenty hot summer days down the hill by the fire hydrant getting wet. Lots of fun in the sun. The water from the hydrant would be so cold flowing all the way to the other side of the street by the gas station. Kids would sit on the front of the hydrant and literally fly across the street due to the strong streams of water. One girl flew so hard across the street during a green light and almost got hit by a bus.

Mona was a very wise child. She would sit in the park on the saddle with a big bag full of snacks watching everything and everybody, cracking jokes with her friends. She didn't miss a beat. She had known Tony for as long as she could remember. As they grew older, the games became more adventurous: Sitting on the pancakes drinking 40's, wine coolers, and Cisco, rolling up bamboo paper and blunts filled with weed, ducking and running from the bats that would appear on the light post, cracking up and scared to death at the same damn time. Cisco was nothing to fuck with either. It was straight crack juice. One bottle of that would have you flat on your ass twisted.

Growing up in the hood during the late 80's was something special. It had its ups and downs but everyone stuck together. Tony became one of Vince's favorites. And Tony's sister Niema hung out with Mona and Kai. Vince taught them everything they knew. They were one big happy family. They belonged to the same team and Vince took Tony under his wing partying at all the hottest clubs with the real OG's.

Vince taught Tony everything about the game, putting him on to all kinds of connects, teaching him the code of the streets early.

He knew that there would be a lot of animosity, but he chose Tony because he saw a lot of potential and character in him. That's what made the clique stand out, all of them. They just had that glow that no one could touch. The more dope they sold, the more money they stacked. A lot of outsiders wanted in and the stakes got real high for a piece of the pie. It was on and popping in the hood. Selling drugs was the name of the game with street credibility and fame. Life is filled with decisions and choices. With those choices come consequences and Mona's family chose the fast life.

VINCE
CHAPTER
Four

Vince opened up the hallway window in the projects happy as fuck! He had a big stack of money and wanted to share every penny. "Aww man Vince, you beat that shit, I'm happy you're home my man." Mickey said to his longtime friend who was throwing thousands of dollars out of the window. "Yeah my man!" "That case is fucking history. They can't stop me. Fuck all these snitches and rat bitches." Vince shouted smiling with bands of money in his hands. It was the first day of school. A beautiful fall day with autumn leaves blowing in the wind. Everybody and they mama wanted a piece of what was flying out of the window. People were running from every direction trying to catch all of the $20's and $50's falling from the building. "Enjoy kids, enjoy." Vince smiled as he looked out of the window in the hallway watching the kids cheering as they happily caught on to the bills flying in the air. "I'm fucking free, fuck all these punk motherfuckers trying to stop me." Vince shouted still smiling in the hallway. It felt like Christmas in the projects! All the kids had a half day at school as they ran up the hill with their eyes wide open. Vince was in a hell of a good mood that day because he actually spent thousands of dollars sharing his joy with all of the people from the hood. "I can't believe it Bro, you made it, you home." Sid spoke as he opened another window to throw more money out. Vince was smiling on the outside because he was free, but on the inside, he didn't know who to trust. Word around the hood was that Vince just beat a serious case in court that could have sent him away for a very long time. Vince just paid his lawyer a great stack of cash for winning his case. "More money, more problems!"

HOOD GAMES

"It's a daily struggle keeping these haters off your back." Vince stated with a big smile on his face. He was a happy man glad to have his freedom. Vince was free of all charges.

Days like these were hard to come by and were truly celebrated. Vince's attire was on point as usual. He was dressed very professionally in his favorite color two-piece gray suit with a burgundy handkerchief in the top pocket. Vince carried a burgundy brief case that complimented his gators. There he was fine as can be standing in the hallway with his goons, popping bottles of Moet and smoking Cuban cigars. Some goons smoked blunts filled with weed and some were laced with coke. Nonetheless, there were bottles by the caseloads ready to be popped.

The aroma of Mrs. Heely's cooking filled the air and made everyone's mouth water. Mrs. Heely was the heart of the projects. This woman was on your side no matter what went down. She would protect you from the cops, feed you and beat the shit out of you all at the same time. Mrs. Heely threw down in the kitchen. Her baked macaroni and cheese just melted in your mouth. Her collard greens and barbecue chicken were out of sight! Everyone stood in line to taste some of her famous sweet potato pie. and You best to believe she made a profit off the shit too. She cooked so fucking good that money was never an issue. It wasn't even discussed. She had big-timers and hustlers doing her food shopping and paying her bills just to keep their bellies filled with her love.

Music was pumping loud out of the speakers in the hallway and everyone was singing along with the record playing. "Satisfaction... Ohhhh! I can't get none Satisfaction..." Vince sang along with the sweet tunes playing out of the speakers. Everyone knew how much Vince loved that song as they all laughed out loud singing along with the record. Everybody was happy and smiling, drinking champagne and cognac, toasting to the good news and having a good ole time. Then, all of a sudden, the elevator sounded for the door to open.

Once the elevator opened, everyone was shocked and surprised to see Vince's brother holding the dude who had enough balls to try and snitch on Vince in court just a week ago. Holmes stood in the elevator shaking like a little bitch. "Well I'll be damned!" Vince snarled, staring at the man his brother was holding. "Where you find this rat?" Vince asked, with his voice all serious.

"Yo! I found his punk ass sitting up in Rochdale movie theatre; ducking and hiding because he saw me coming." Justice answered, holding the man by his collar. Justice shouted "You know I wanted so badly to peel his cap back; but I knew you'd love to do the honors on this one yourself." He smiled from ear- to- ear, proud that he had found the man that tried to get his brother locked up.

"Oh! "You got that one right," Vince snarled rubbing his palms together. "Ayo! Bring his ass over here. Now!" Vince roared as his brother brought the crying man to the center of the hallway. After being thrown out of the elevator, you could hear the man's fear from his cries. Vince hadn't even touched him and his face was already wet with tears and he was begging and pleading for his safety. "Shut the fuck up Duke!" Vince shouted. "You weren't crying and carrying on when the police asked your punk ass to testify against me. And you damn sure wasn't crying in court when you looked me straight in the face and lied on my name. You didn't cry then did you? Did you?!" Vince asked the man while putting a cigar out on his face. The poor man screamed like a little toddler as the embers burned his cheek. The music was still pumping in the hallway and a crowd of friends and family was standing there, eyes wide open, with drinks in hand. Then Vince came out of nowhere and cracked an unopened bottle of Moet on Duke's head. He grabbed him by the ear and pulled him into the elevator with blood running down his face. When they arrived downstairs in the lobby, Vince dragged the man outside on his knees.

Duke's pants ripped around the knee caps as he was dragged along. The blood just poured out of the sockets as Vince continued dragging him down the hill. Little kids began running down the hill behind the screaming man, grabbing his sneakers from his feet and throwing them up in the air so they could catch on to the phone wires in the middle of the street. There was a trail of blood coming from the building to the bottom of the hill. The man begged for his life pleading with Vince to let him go. "I didn't do it I swear. Please don't kill me. I didn't do it." The poor man begged for mercy with snots and tears running down his face.

"Fuck you bitch. You know exactly what you did motherfucker. Now you're about to feel the pain." Vince had to place duck-tape onto the screaming man's mouth to stop from attracting any more unnecessary attention.

Vince's goons tied Duke's ass to a tree with nothing but his drawers on. Then went upstairs to Mrs. Heely's apartment to retrieve Vince's gun. When they returned, Vince had already thrown a bucket of cold water on the man, making sure his body was nice and wet. After wetting him, Vince began beating him with a belt. Once Vince started, his goons joined in, whipping the poor man and whelping his skin until the belts ripped into his flesh. His cries sounded like a wounded animal from under the tape. Vince stopped beating Duke and ripped the tape off of his mouth. Soon as Duke had the chance, he started screaming as loud as he could for help when Vince walked up and smacked him in the face with the butt of his gun. He was knocked out at the bottom of the hill tied up to a tree.

After untying his helpless, bleeding body, Vince's goons wrapped him up in a blanket and placed him into the trunk of one of the cars that were parked down the hill. Homeboy stayed inside of that trunk practically all night while Vince and his family ate dinner, celebrated and partied hard, forgetting that he was even in there.

After celebrating, Vince peeled off in his BMW with one of his chicks and ordered his goons to take care of that problem in the trunk. Vince was gone for the night and so was his snitch.

"Oh shit! That was the first time I ever saw Vince that angry," Kai shouted with her eyes wide open, talking to the girls in her clique.

"I don't blame him, shit, that motherfucker had it coming. He threatened Vince's freedom by snitching on him the way that he did. If he was smart, he would have taken his ass out of town somewhere instead of sitting up in the fucking movies. Eating popcorn and shit, like shit is sweet," Niema replied with an attitude as she puffed on her weed. The girls agreed with Niema as she passed her blunt to their friend Kizz, laughing about how Duke was being dragged around like a little rag doll. After that day, no one dared to mention or speak of that particular incident ever again. They all knew that sometimes things are better off when they are left alone...

SCHOOL DAYZ

CHAPTER
Five

"*I thought this class would never end.*" Kai thought to herself as she heard the school bell ringing with a look of relief on her caramel face. Standing on the steps of Hillcrest high school was a tall girl very petite with a freckle filled button nose waiting patiently for her friend to exit the school building. Kai was a good, genuine person but always stayed with a few tricks up her sleeve. Things seemed to always ride easy with Kai. She inherited that trait from her mother who was a free-spirited person.

Kai walked without a care in the world, always smiling. "What's up girl?" Uma yelled through the crowd of students as she approached her friend.

"Ain't nothing girl," Kai answered, smiling and eating a pineapple icy. Both girls were dipped for the day and shining in the sun's light. Kai sported a pink and white Puma suit with spanking white Puma's. And Uma wore a skin-tight Adidas suit with some matching black and white Adidas.

They both wore their hair in flat twists with door knocker earrings in their ears. "I'm just sitting here debating on whether I should go to this last class or not that's all," Kai said, finishing her icy throwing it into the trashcan on the corner.

After Kai finished talking, Uma shouted, "Yo! Let me tell you what the fuck went down during my lunch period. You missed it." Uma chuckled, while she talked almost choking on her words.

"You so silly girl, what happened?" Kai asked smiling.

"You remember that bitch we had an argument with a couple of weeks ago at the mall?" Uma asked. "I think she's in your gym class."

Kai replied "Yeah," while thinking to herself 'That bitch's name is Lena or some shit. Yo fuck that bitch, what happened?' "What she do now?"

"I was standing in line at lunch today talking to Leslie, you know the chick that does our hair." Kai agreed, nodding her head up and down as she signaled Uma to finish telling her the story. "Well, I was asking Leslie if she could re-do my twists for me next week or whatever, you know we just kicking it on the line and shit. Then here comes this bitch Lena, squeezing her little ugly ass in between Leslie and her sister on the line bumping Leslie hard on her shoulder."

"Oh no she didn't that bitch is bold!" Kai screamed.

Then Uma yelled "Yeah I don't know what was up with her this morning, but she must have had a hangover from drinking too much of that liquor last night, ole' drunken bitch." Uma rolled her eyes while she continued. "Anyway, you know how Leslie's temper is, so Leslie said to the bitch 'Hold up I know you didn't just come over her squeezing your ugly ass in the middle of our conversation minding our business. Get the fuck from out of my space,' knocking Lena down flat on her ass.

55

The whole lunchroom was screaming and laughing in tears on how that bitch landed on the floor."

"Oh my goodness, you serious. Leslie did that?" Kai asked her friend giggling.

"Yes girl," Uma answered "But that's not it."

"When the bitch fell, she had the nerve to drop her juice on the floor causing it to splatter all over my mother fuckin Adidas. Now you know a bitch was heated then, but I just let her sorry ass lay right there on the floor to finish the show she started. I know one thing for sure," Uma firmly said after finishing her story.

"What's that?" Kai asked as both girls glanced down at Uma's new kicks.

Uma shouted "Let that bitch approach me one more time and I swear I'm gonna get little Mona and them to come up here and whip that bitch ass, you watch and see."

"Now you know Kai, if one of us start stomping on that bitch's tail, she'd end up right in the emergency room. Little Mona can come up here and whip her ass in the same fashion and no one will know where it came from."

"You've got a point there Uma, I see you've been doing your homework up in them classrooms scheming on how you gonna redden that bitch's tail without even touching her. It ain't no need in getting expelled from school over some lame bitch who can't even keep her fuckin balance." Both girls remained silent collecting their thoughts to themselves enjoying the breeze.

It was no longer than five minutes of silence when both Kai and Uma were interrupted by a crowd of people screaming and carrying on up the hill across the street from their school. The two girls ran anxiously toward the crowd. Kai wondered what could have happened now after what Uma just told her. "What happened?" Kai asked a young fellah she knew standing out of the crowd laughing to himself and shaking his head from side to side.

Kai and Uma could hardly catch their breath when the young fellah hollered, "You ought to know Kai, don't act like you stupid now." Kai and Uma looked at each other in shock.

"What the fuck you mean she ought to know motherfucker?" Uma screamed at the top of her lungs, her face filled with anger.

The young fellah saw the anger building up in Uma's eyes and shouted "Alright- alright, your little sister Mona and some chick over there kicking Lena's ass that's what happened. I was just playing around with you because I thought you already knew what time it was. Now that I see you don't, my bad," the fellah shouted out sarcastically as he walked away from the crowd back to the school, still laughing out loud.

By this time, Kai was confused, wondering how on earth did Mona have time to even come up to her school when she was just learning of the situation herself. And why wasn't she in school? Although Kai was furious with Mona, both she and Uma rushed through the crowd to help her. As the two girls pushed their way through the crowd, they both heard the loud screams coming from Lena, begging and screaming, as she yelled, "Get these bitches off me!!"

The whole school had surrounded the fight. Kai finally reached an opening to find Lena sprawled out on the ground with her clothes covered in blood, screaming bloody murder.

Her head was full of bald spots from Mona on top of her pulling out every strand. And trying to scratch her eyeballs out at the same time. She just kept repeating herself over and over again, "Step in my way again bitch, step in my way again." Lena had no idea as to what Mona meant. All she wanted was for Mona to get the fuck up off her. Finally, after struggling with Mona, unwrapping her hands from Lena's bald head, all four girls fell directly on top of Lena staining each other's clothes and laughing at the same time.

"What the hell are you doing here Mona? Why aren't you in school," Kai asked her little sister as they were interrupted by the sound of police sirens coming towards the school.

"Shit! She'll explain herself later. Let's just get the fuck out of here first," Uma shouted. The girls picked themselves up from the ground leaving poor Lena to scream as loud as she could for help. Kai grabbed Mona and the four girls ran like hell down the hill, in the opposite direction of the sirens. They were running so fast that they almost made it back to the projects. The girls then started to slow down to catch their breath from running so fast when a black Wrangler pulls up next to them.

Staring with his eyes wide open, the radio blasting in his ride, was Kai's cousin Boone. "What the fuck happened to y'all?" Boone asked, covering up his seats with some towels from his trunk before letting the girls in.

"Well whatever's going on with you girls, I'm behind y'all, but I'll be damned if I let you bitches fuck up my ride. Get in the car!" Boone shouted. As soon as the girls piled up into the car, Uma told Boone to bring them to her boyfriend's crib.

Uma's boyfriend was out of town for a few days but she had a spare key to his pad. So she could lay low over there if she wanted until he returned. He also had asked her to feed his fish for him and handle some other necessities. Uma had been having a lot of problems at home due to the constant fights and arguments she had with her father. Her dad's new girlfriend hated her and had started pitting Uma's dad against her. Things had gotten so bad with her dad that Kai asked her family if Uma could stay with them until she got on her feet. Since then she'd been living between her boyfriend and Kai's family. "Look at my fucking clothes," Kai screamed. "Today is just not my day. How the fuck you find out so fast about what happened today?" Kai asked Mona. "What bird flew over to inform you like you so damn important?"

"Oh, Leslie's little sister paged Kema on her pager and when Kema called her back, she had told us everything that Lena did. And at the same time, we were getting out of school too because we had a half day today," Mona replied, lying through her teeth.

"Oh!" Kai answered, rolling her eyes. The girls finally made it to Uma's boyfriend's crib. Her boyfriend lived on a nice little cozy block in Briarwood, on some down low shit. Once they made it inside, Uma checked around the place to make sure the coast was clear. Then she began ripping off her bloody clothes as her friends followed her moves.

Uma collected all the clothes and dumped them into the washing machine.

Kema finally opened her mouth and yelled "Look what I got." Pulling out a large leather Fendi bag from out of her book bag.

"What is it?" Mona asked.

"Oh, like you don't fucking know," Kema snarled looking at Mona like she was stupid. Mona didn't reply. When Kema emptied the contents of the bag they all were in shock. They were all sitting there, mouths wide open, staring at the table filled with Lena and her sister's jewelry. There sat 4 pair of door knockers, 3 bangle bracelets, a gold nugget watch and a phat rope chain with a piece on it.

"Now that's what she gets for trying to be cute today," Kai giggled trying on her new chain.

"I bet she won't be getting in your way anymore," Mona smiled while dancing to the song that played on the radio.

Kema added "If she's smart, she won't even look at y'all asses." The girls split the jewels and returned to school as if nothing happened; only to be turned around to the Dean's office. Kai and Uma had gotten expelled from school for one week and had to stay up to fifty feet away from Lena. She had gotten an order of protection against each girl. She couldn't prove to the cops about the jewels, because it was basically her word against theirs.

They were off the hook because Lena was too damn scared to do anything. Luckily for them, her being so frightened stopped the girls from getting locked up. Stepping out of the school together, Kai and Uma walked down the stairs and down the hill towards the bus stop. While they waited for the bus, Uma tapped Kai on the shoulder and said, "Mona better not bring her grown ass up here fucking up our rep ever again." Both girls laughed together, knowing damn well that they would be into some shit real soon. But for the moment, they just needed some space to breath...

SASHA

CHAPTER
Six

"Where you think you going, dressed like a hot cake that ain't been flipped yet? What's so fucking important out there that you have to wear all of that makeup caked up on your face like some hooker, huh?" Sasha's mother asked while she chopped up some green peppers and onions for the stewed chicken she was preparing for dinner.

"Calm down Mama, I told you that my boss changed my hours and gave me the night shift. And you know the extra money helps out around here and puts food on the table when we need it; so I don't see what the big fuss is over," Sasha squealed.

"The big fuss is, shit, I ain't seen a check yet huh," her mother shouted. "Strolling up in here with them fancy tight clothes on, at all times of the morning, knowing you have a young baby at home that needs you. You haven't spent any time with that girl in over two weeks due to your busy schedule."

"I hope you not out there selling your body in them streets Sasha because you damn sure ain't gonna be bringing that shit up in here. I'm not taking care of no more children. No more you hear!"

Sasha's mother yelled as loud as she possibly could to get through to her daughter before she left the house. Slamming the door behind her, Sasha stomped down the stairs and was gone to face another night of work. Sasha had told her mother that she worked at a fine restaurant out in Manhattan that stayed open 24 hours a day.

Sasha explained to her mother that her boss needed her for the night shift because she was so reliable. Mentioning that would put her mother at ease, until she would get caught wearing one of her skimpy outfits again. The restaurant she mentioned is nothing of the sort and hardly in her calendar. Sasha was a hostess at a strip joint and turned tricks every now and then when necessary. Sasha was very beautiful and she used her beauty to her advantage. Sasha had been feeling down for the last couple of weeks because she knew that she hadn't been spending enough time with her new baby.

Who else would put food on the table if she did stay home? Her mother hadn't been working in over three years due to her disability and the checks she received from it hardly pay the bills. Working over at the strip joint paid the rent and then some. Sasha had the prettiest costumes, fine jewelry, colorful minks and leathers. This girl definitely rolled out in style wherever she went. Driving in a navy blue chromed out Benz, with tan leather interior seats cruising through the midtown tunnel; Sasha watched the clock making sure she wasn't late for her shift. While listening to Salt and Pepa's *Push It*, Sasha screamed "Push it real good!"

As soon as she reached the end of the tunnel, her Motorola cell phone rang. Reaching into her handbag and pressing the receiver, "Hello," Sasha answered softly.

"Yeah baby, I've been waiting up at the joint for over 45 minutes. What's the hold-up?" Jim asked.

"I'm sorry baby, you know I want to look my best for you sweetheart and time is beauty," Sasha answered smiling in the mirror.

Jim shouted "Well the last time I checked, time is also my money! So, I'd appreciate it if you brought your sexy light ass up here and get some of this good money before one of these hoes in here gets it for you."

There was a dial tone at the end of the receiver and Sasha was left on the other end with her mouth wide open and horns beeping at her to move from out of the intersection. Starting the job as a hostess, was the only task that Sasha was to perform. Her boss hired her because he thought she would bring in good clientele and dancing wasn't in Sasha's forte anyway. After a few months flew by and the customers started rolling in, Sasha thought that she could make some big money of her own on the side with the customers she lured in each night in addition to the base salary she received hosting and she did just that. Sasha was well known throughout the projects.

She and her mother lived right up the street across from the deli. Her mother's brother became a big-time hustler and wound up doing a lot of business in the projects through Vince. So for Sasha not to be affiliated with people in the projects became impossible. She would have to travel through the projects every single day after school when she was a young girl. Sasha made it known that she turned a few tricks on the down low to a few hustlers in the hood.

Their tips alone paid off her rent, car note and clothing for months every time she fucked around. She never was disrespected because her head game was off the hook.

She could suck a dick so good and make it disappear in her mouth like a magician. Sasha had doctors, lawyers, pimps, customers from the joint and hustlers in the hood sweating her from every direction. Sasha finally entered the club to find her boss waiting on tables with a stern look on his face. She hurried to the dressing room to prepare herself for the night. She changed into her sexy costume and tucked everything into place. Wearing 4-inch high heels, Sasha eased herself behind the bar. The strip joint was dimly lit with disco lights rolling everywhere. There was a big screen TV placed directly where the bar was so the customers were entertained with music and adult videos.

Long poles were on the stage for the dancers to perform on and there were about ten different booths, with customers piled in each one. After squinting her eyes around the club, Sasha finally noticed Jim sitting at one of the booths with champagne glasses filled with Moet and hoes all around him. "Can I help you?" Sasha asked the gentleman who was surrounded by women, with a sexy tone in her voice.

"Oh shit! You surely can. Go and get me some more champagne and here baby, this is for you," Jim whispered, tucking a hundred-dollar bill into Sasha's bra. "And There's plenty more where that came from," Jim mentioned slapping Sasha on the ass and lusting over her huge firm breasts. Sasha just loved the sound of Jim's deep voice.

She knew that he lusted over her and would give her everything she wanted. After getting the champagne, Sasha returned to the booth to find the curtain closed with Jim behind it sitting there with his pants unzipped. Sasha eased behind the booth and gave her best customer what he desired. Jim loved the way Sasha sucked his dick. No matter how hard Jim tried to please her, or how much money that he or other customers gave her; Sasha always felt the urge to take a little more to ease her discomfort.

Whenever Sasha serviced Jim, she always found the right time to peel off about $300 or more of his stash each time she saw him. He wouldn't know the difference no way, because her head game was so good that it made him lose track of his pockets. And all those bottles of Moet he consumed made him too stoned to notice anything else Sasha had done. The club was very crowded when Sasha returned from her private venture with her customer. Sasha's boss didn't notice her gone because he was busy watching the dancers on stage and she already had a girl covering for her at the bar until she returned.

Music was bumping and naked women were bouncing everywhere. Giving lap dances and teasing poles. *'Aww Shit! It's really hot up in the joint tonight,'* Vince thought to himself as he made his way through the crowd of men lusting over the hoes on stage. Vince didn't like walking around with a bunch of goons, so he kept his distance to keep the attention off of him. As soon as Vince approached the bar, he became the life of the party. Everyone knew he was in the joint now. Vince shouted "Two rounds of champagne on me," as a crowd of hoes purred and hollered.

66

"And you," Vince ordered snapping his fingers, "Bring me three bottles of Moet to my table," pointing to Sasha. Sasha was pleased because she always wanted a piece of Vince's cream. Vince came to the joint fresh wearing a jet-black pimp hat laced with a silver feather that complimented his silver handkerchief with a jet-black pantsuit and some crisp black gators. Fine as he wanted to be, chilling with his goons. Vince rarely came out to the joint because he was so use to being pampered by hoes that it didn't make a bit of difference.

He knew what he wanted, and looking at Sasha's voluptuous body, he had made his choice. Sasha knew that Vince meant business and she was to cater to his every fantasy. By the time Sasha's boss noticed her sweating Vince, he could give a fuck as long as the money kept flowing through. She was just as good as any other hoe in the joint. Regular customers were to stay down stairs by the booth or at the bar. Customers like Vince got the royal treatment upstairs in VIP at the master suite with a warm Jacuzzi and King sized water beds. Vince let his goons know that he would be up in the master suite for an hour and to stay put in the vicinity of the club until he was through. Understanding their boss's every word, Vince's goons relaxed and partied hard until they were needed.

Inside the suite was very romantic. Vince sat at the mini bar while he awaited Sasha's entrance. Sasha on the other hand wanted everything to be perfect. She had changed into her sexiest outfit revealing all the goods and slipped into some matching furry high heels. Vince made a drink for Sasha and himself when Sasha made her way into the suite. Vince was amazed at her beauty as she danced for him in the middle of the room.

HOOD GAMES

Sasha began teasing and touching her body removing every piece of clothing she had on leaving her voluptuous ass and breasts visible.

Vince walked up to her and made his presence known by pulling her close to him. Kissing her full wet lips and not letting go, sweeping her off her feet. Sasha was feeling sensations all through her body that no man had ever made her feel. They continued to kiss falling on top of the large water bed bouncing everywhere. Vince became overwhelmed when Sasha discovered his manhood and began sucking it uncontrollably. He couldn't believe the view of Sasha's lips making his manhood disappear before his eyes. Sasha sucked Vince dick like a warrior, with her tits in the air. When Vince could no longer resist the urge, he grabbed Sasha by the hair and fucked her at full speed causing her to reach the biggest orgasm she'd ever had.

They both fell at the same time with smiles of satisfaction on their faces. Vince signaled Sasha to get dressed as she begged to see him again. He agreed, promising her another night of pleasure. Sasha showered and dressed in a separate bathroom from Vince. She was shocked to see how much money she peeled off his wad of cash. and She really hoped he didn't notice anything different. Sasha had $1200 after counting the $300 she copped from Jim, plus the $200 he had already given her. Then receiving $300 before servicing Vince and peeled $400 from him. Sasha smiled as she stuffed the money into her bra.

Stepping back into the suite, Sasha couldn't believe her eyes. "What's going on?" Sasha looked so scared as she continued to ask Vince stupid questions which she knew the answers to. She was totally in shock to see Vince standing in the middle of the room with all of his goons.

Vince just looked at her and snarled "You tell me bitch. I see you've been having a little problem with those fingers of yours. They kind of sticky, huh?" Vince asked angrily pacing around the room.

"What kills me is that you have the best head in the world and I know a few pimps who could use a trick like you." Sasha couldn't believe what she was hearing. Vince shouted "I hope you weren't planning on leaving without me getting my money's worth." Pulling Sasha by the hair and yanking her head back, Vince then whispered "I would have given you the world. Dirty bitch! Shooting this bitch is too fucking easy, I'll be at the lounge when you're done." He threw her on the bed, letting her keep the cash she stole.

As Vince left the joint, you could hear the loud screams coming from the master suite. No one dared to say a word to Vince because they did not want to feel his wrath. Vince's goons then paid Sasha's boss and a few hoes a wad of cash to keep their mouths shut about Sasha's disappearance as they carried her kicking and screaming out of the strip club. Everything in the hood remained the same as if nothing happened.

Except for the everyday questions and assumptions from Sasha's mother who searched the whole hood ripping and ranting, cursing everybody in sight worried about her only daughter. Sasha's mother searched for weeks for the whereabouts of her daughter until one day the police found her tricking on the track uptown near West Side Highway, skied up still wearing her finest outfit ever.

Sasha took a beating that left her in la-la land. After being fed to the sharks and pimps, she just wasn't ever the same. Sasha's mother was crushed because her daughter was pimped out and lost to the streets, leaving her to care for her baby as if she never had one. Sasha's appearance changed drastically looking hard and ran down. Living life in the fast lane has never been easy. And by the looks of Sasha, it's a hard and bumpy road. I guess good looks weren't used to the best of her ability after all.

THE CLIQUE

CHAPTER
Seven

"Damn this shit is taking forever," Mona squealed to herself while she wiped the sweat from off her forehead.

"Well if you would just shut up and concentrate on your stash, maybe we can finish a little faster," Kema screamed shooting her friend a glare.

"Both of y'all need to shut the fuck up! Don't none of you little motherfuckers belong here no way," Kai shouted while she placed some white powder into a small bundle. The girls had one day out of the week to bag up 2 kilos of coke for one of the big-timers at the spot. Since Thursday was skating night at Laces Roller Skating Rink, the girls chose to bag up every Thursday morning. That way they'd be finished in time to collect their pay and get fresh for the jump off later that night.

They used their friend Sierra's crib to conduct business, since her mom worked all day and didn't get home until late night. Sierra didn't work with her girls that morning because she chose to go and get her boots knocked as usual. Sierra loved to fuck! She was very attractive with long red hair and had a nice body also. Si-Si stayed fresh every day too.

She had the hots for one of the big-timers they worked for and chose to go and fuck him every Thursday, instead of sweating hard with the girls. I guess she thought she had it like that because it was her house that was being used to bag that shit up in the first place. She was getting paid for that regardless. So Sierra would disappear every time the girls met up at the building.

The Clique skipped one day of school out the week to make that paper stack. Niema and Kizz would stay outside by the basketball courts down the hill to look out for any suspicious motherfuckers who thought they knew about their dealings. The two chose to stay outside because Kizz just couldn't stand the smell of the coke. It was just too strong for her to bear. Their boss gave her and Niema the lookout job since they were always together.

Kizz's light complexion just shined in the sun. Wearing a fresh pair of Puma's and pun-pun shorts, she was staring at the new gold nugget bracelet her man brought her. Niema on the other hand was a brown skinned cutie wearing an acid washed jean mini skirt with some spanking white Air Nikes and a fresh sweat shirt from Mr. Lee. They both wore their hair in tiny box braids, as Kizz waited calmly for her friend to twist her hair up in a ponytail so she could put her rope chain on. Pay day for each girl was $600 each for every kilo bagged.

Sometimes they'd get stuck with an extra kilo of coke depending on how fast the shit been selling. They would end up getting paid a triple salary and today was damn sure one of those days. Each girl was paid the same amount of money at the same exact time so there would be no confusion whatsoever.

Each job was very important and the girls took their jobs very seriously and for that, they were well taken care of. Shit! Being paid that type of money in the late 80's was crazy. Especially for as young as these chicks were. Kizz, Niema and Kai were all in high school. Mona, Kema and Sierra were in junior high. The attention they received in school was off the hook.

Mona and Kema went to the same school, but always ended up at Kai's school getting into some shit they had no business being in. Every single day each girl was dressed in their freshest kicks and had an outfit to match each pair. They sported them Reebok classics in every color. They rocked Pumas, Cortez Nikes, Adidas, Fila, New Balance and you can't forget them Lotto's. With all the little colorful patches. These chicks had every kick you could think of and wore it well. Their jewels were off the hook too. They all had puffed swirls and doorknocker earrings and on occasion, they would switch shit up and wear the big dolphin earrings or diamond hoops.

They all wore gold fronts on their teeth. Kai and Mona wore bottom frames, while Niema and Kizz wore tops. All girls in the Clique sported them butter leather and goose bombers, sheep skin shearlings and 8-ball jackets. Mona even sported a 7- ball, fresh to death. Each girl had a different color snorkel so they stood out from all the rest of the hood rats because those bitches could never see paper like the Clique stacked. After finishing work for the day, they all met up down the hill with their bundles at the spot. Made their transactions, collected their cash and then jetted over to Jamaica Avenue to cop some gear for the jump off that evening in Niema's boyfriend's navy blue BM.

After shopping, they all went and got their hair and nails done and then made it over to Margherita's for a tasty slice of pizza. While eating, Kizz started explaining a situation that she and Niema had gotten into in the projects with three birds while waiting down the hill by the courts today at work. Mona and Kema kind of knew something was up because Kizz never walked around without her jewels unless it was beef. Kizz began explaining how she and Niema had gone to the frank truck on the corner to have a quick break since there hadn't been anybody around the hood at the time. Both girls ordered two knishes stuffed with chili and sodas.

When all of a sudden, three bitches walked up behind them. They knew the broads from around the way. They lived in the projects also, but never had any altercations with one another because Niema and Kizz always had other things on the brain then to be thinking about some chicken heads clocking them. After Kizz ordered her food and collected her change; she continued her conversation with Niema when one of the broads named Dana came out of nowhere and bumped Kizz hard causing her food to smear onto her brand new sweatshirt.

Kizz stopped in her tracks to collect her thoughts. She then removed her jewels and handed her food and jewelry to Niema charging straight into the direction of the bitch that bumped her and punched her right in her grill bussing her lip wide open. All of a sudden, the commotion had gotten very loud and the guys at the spot noticed Kizz scrapping so they all ran across the street to stop the shit before the broad who bumped Kizz could hit her back. They both kicked and argued knowing that they wouldn't be fighting until they both met up again under different circumstances.

74

As both girls returned back to the courts, Kizz couldn't believe how that bitch Dana tried to play her. She kept seeing visions of Dana's face filled with blood for the rest of her shift. This kind of thinking wasn't at all normal for Kizz, because she was genuinely nice inside and out. Their boss was furious to find out Kizz was fighting and causing unnecessary attention, but was informed that she wasn't the cause. Kizz could give a fuck because her lip wasn't busted no way! She told that bitch the next time she saw her she was going to stomp a mud hole knee deep in that ass, straight up.

The girls were in shock sitting there at the table seeing Kizz so angry because she was usually all smiles and happy to look as good as she did. "Damn Kizz! I can't believe that shit went down the way it did," Kai responded eating her slice of pizza.

"I'm fucking tight right now! I'ma get that bitch. When I catch her, I'ma beat the shit out of her fucking ass." Kizz snarled as she put her braids up into a bun. After Kizz shared the news with the rest of her Clique, all the girls were prepared for the worse once they saw them bitches. Since everyone was going skating that night, they knew just how to handle them hoes. Laces was one of the hottest skating joints out. Where everyone from Uptown to Queens met to chill and floss all night long. It was like a mini Skate Key. Playas from all over were at the rink tonight. Mercedes and Jeeps were everywhere in sight. A few Kats pulled up in drop tops with their chicks inside.

Tony and his crew pulled up behind Vince and his goons. Shit was about to jump off. Everybody was dipped, wearing rope chains and pinky rings just off the hook.

HOOD GAMES

The Clique pulled up in two separate rides. Kai drove with Mona and Kema in her man's Mercedes wagon. While Niema drove with Kizz and Sierra in her man's navy blue BM. All were dipped to perfection. Kai, Kizz and Niema wore their miniskirts. White, black and navy blue with skin tight tank tops to match. While Mona, Kema and Sierra wore tight jeans and tops in the same colors. Hair and nails tight, jewels shining and everything was as good as ever. Music was jumping as they checked their shoes in to receive their skates for the evening. Looking around the rink, Mona noticed everyone having a good time and in good spirits. Vince and Tony gathered at a table over by the bar with his goons in the mix, drinking Champagne and toasting to their favorite jam that was playing. While putting on their skates, the girls could hear Tony singing to his song, *"Keep Rising to the top! Give it all you got!"* All the girls burst out laughing as they tied their laces. Each girl rolled over to the pretzel stand to get some lemonade and something to snack on and then rolled onto the rink to do a few rounds.

The DJ was playing all the latest jams like *"It Takes Two!"* and *"Ain't No Half Steppin!"* Shit was on and popping. Ladies flirted hard with the fellas on the floor, doing all the latest dance moves skating backwards and forwards around the rink when Kai noticed Kema falling off balance, sliding down the rink and bumping her back onto the hard wall.

Looking around, Mona and Kai saw that Niema and Kizz were still rolling around the rink unaware of what occurred. While they helped Kema to her feet and onto the main floor, Kema had explained how that bitch Dana was out on the skating rink and how she just cut her off causing her to fall.

76

Mona and Kai then rushed back onto the rink to find the rest of the Clique. Sierra had already gotten off to talk to one of her fuck buddies. Si-Si did anything to avoid a fight on any given day, word! Making their way back around the rink, Mona saw that Kema had already made her way back around before them and she was holding the bitch who cut her off over in the corner.

While approaching the girls, Kizz was already finishing what Dana started earlier in the projects that day. The chick who cut Kema off at the rink was the same bitch who bumped Kizz by the courts that morning Kizz was filled with rage holding onto the pole while kicking that bitch in her grill with all her might. No one could quite notice what was going on because the rink was packed and the music was so loud that it kept the skaters in rotation blocking the whole scene in the corner.

Each girl took turns kicking and punching, when Kizz grabbed her skate and began bashing the broad in the face with it. Dana's friends were nowhere in sight. There was one chick she was skating with standing on the sidelines shook, just watching Dana get her ass kicked. Those the type of bitches you can't even rock with no day of the week. Finally, Kizz gave up swinging when she saw that Dana was bleeding profusely from her face and head and the crowd began to notice the commotion. The Clique skated back into the crowd and began to observe with everyone else while Kizz rushed off to the restroom to wash the blood off of the skate.

When she stepped out of the bathroom, she noticed Vince talking to the owner of the rink. Vince conducted several business deals with the Italians who owned the skating rink.

So Vince felt the need to explain that Kizz was one of his own and that nothing was to be said about what she has done or there would be major repercussions.

The owner understood Vince immediately. Everyone in Laces that night was shocked and amazed as they watched the poor girl being rolled out of the rink hollering and screaming on a stretcher with her friends running behind her into the ambulance. Dana suffered ten stitches to the top of her head due to the blows from the skate. The crowd lessened after the fight ended, but people still partied hard until about 3am.

After leaving the skating rink, everybody who was somebody met up at the after-hour spot for a bite to eat at Lucille's Diner. Lucille's made delicious cheeseburgers with fried onions. That's exactly what the girls ordered along with fries, sides of onion rings and a half and half fruit punch/ lemonade for everyone. Everybody enjoyed their food, laughing and giggling about the happenings of the night, when Sierra squeezed her way out of the booth making her way downstairs to the bathroom. Exiting the restroom, Sierra decided to use the pay phone before going back upstairs.

She noticed two guys having an argument by the men's room, but she continued to make her phone call. The only thing Sierra could think about was some dick. She was fucked up from drinking and smoking all night and she didn't want to go home until somebody's manhood was deep inside of her. As Sierra popped her gum, she danced real sexy while the phone rang. Sierra stood on the other end of the receiver awaiting pleasure, when she saw the two guys who were arguing approaching her. Sierra slept on her thoughts and continued her sexy mood.

"Don't fucking move bitch!" The gunman said, silently clicking the phone she was on pointing a fully loaded 9mm handgun into her face. Sierra remained quiet! Then the robber whispered "Give me your fucking jewels bitch! I want everything you got on and don't get cute either or I will blow your motherfucking brains out." Moving quickly, Sierra began removing all of her jewelry starting with her door knockers, to her swirls, down to her bracelets and rings placing it all into a paper bag.

As the gunman robbed Sierra, he had his back turned from the stairway. In the same moment, Tony had gotten up from the booth he was sitting at, to use the men's room. As soon as Tony turned the corner to reach the stairway, he saw Sierra getting robbed, with a gun right before her eyes. Tony then moved backwards, signaling his boys. He put them on to what was happening downstairs, then waited to make his move. Tony removed his gun from his waist side and headed back towards the stairs.

Sierra was crying and scared for her life when she saw Tony making his way down the steps in full speed. He tried not to make any eye contact with Sierra as he approached the gunman, blowing his head clean off and leaving blood to splatter all over Sierra's face and clothes. Without blinking, Sierra picked up the brown paper bag filled with her jewels and took off running. Flying up the steps screaming like a bat out of hell. "They shooting', they shooting'," Sierra screamed, frantically calling out to her friends with blood all over her. The other gunman, who was still down stairs, started shooting at Tony and Sierra missing every shot.

As Tony and Sierra ran up the stairwell, the gunman still rang out shots grazing Sierra in the leg. By this time, Tony and Sierra had just made it up the stairs and people were screaming and running out of the diner. When the gunman made it up the stairs, one of Vince's goons was waiting for him in the cut and fired three shots to his chest, causing him to fall back down the stairs to join his dead friend. Everybody jetted to their rides and onto the freeway, heading back to the projects.

While driving back to the projects, Sierra noticed her leg was bleeding and thought she had gotten shot. Everyone in the car with her started screaming just as loud as she was. When the girls reached the emergency room, they all were relieved to hear that Sierra's leg had only been grazed and it just needed to be cleaned and bandaged, nothing major. Sierra was very lucky to have her life. If it wasn't for Tony, she'd be dead right now! Every now and then, the girls would tease her from time to time whenever she would get into one of her fucking moods.

Sierra still remained the same, but she'd think twice about going places all alone that's for sure. Although Kizz and the girls beat a bitch senseless and Sierra was grazed in the leg and almost robbed of everything she owned, they still managed to have a good night. Even though no one was able to make it to school the next day, they all learned a valuable lesson.

LADY

CHAPTER
Eight

"God grant me the serenity to accept the things I cannot change, courage to change the things, that I can and the wisdom to know the difference. Amen!" Mia said.' Every night Kai, Mona and Mia prayed to the Lord, asking Him for strength and guidance.

"Did you finish your homework Mia? Let me check it before you go to bed," Lady asked while she washed the dishes, listening to Regina Belle on the radio. Their mother taught them to be strong young women no matter how hard things had gotten. She also taught them to always believe and be themselves in any given situation. Lady was beautiful!

Her cinnamon complexion was flawless and she looked like she walked on air. She was tall with long jet black hair that hung down her back. Her oval shaped eyes were brown and she just loved to bat her lashes. Kai and her sisters adored their mother so much. Lady's three girls didn't want for nothing.

Lady worked really hard to keep a roof over their heads and clothes on their backs. She found a new job working as an administrative assistant for many years after Daddy passed away. She pushed a light blue coupe with the name Lady written on the license plate.

Inside her car was laced with navy blue interior leather seats. Her system was navy blue and tan, shit was tight. Lady was shown mad respect in the hood and she always gave it in return. She had a lot of friends and Vince was one of them. They both became very close after her husband passed away. Vince liked Lady a lot. They both had a mutually respectful relationship that no one could understand. Vince and Lady's friendship wasn't sexual at all. They both enjoyed one another's company and Vince needed a good friend that he could talk to. Vince treated her daughters as if they were his own. Lady didn't hang out much and was very conservative about everything. Lady walked down the hill dressed in slacks and high heels ready for a new day at work.

It was hot as hell outside; sprinklers were running and kids were in the park with water filled buckets just dunking each other and carrying on. The basketball court consumed the whole Clique.   All the girls were out in their freshest gear, hoping to not get wet that morning by one of them bad ass kids up the hill in the park.

The girls watched Kai and Mona's mom get into her car, pulling out of the parking space headed for work waving her off as they sat down the hill not saying a word to one another. Everyone was feeling real fucked up for a minute because they missed seeing Vince's face around the hood, just flossing in his BM and shit. Vince had gotten locked up by the police up in Harlem, during a big dope deal gone wrong, the night before last.

"This shit is so fucked up. I can't believe he is gone. I'm going to miss that man he was like a father to me. Damn!" Mona cried talking to her girls in the park.

It seemed so strange without his presence, but he was well taken care of in the pen and had a visit every weekend from his main chick. She kept him aware of all business transactions throughout the hood and brought him food, clothing and commissary. You know all the personal shit a man needs to stay up and hold his head in the cell.

Things weren't looking to good on Vince's end though. Every single day that went by, the police linked Vince to more and more homicides. No one in the hood cared about the allegations against him because in the hood he was the King. Vince was family filled with genuine love and trust. He wasn't like the monster the cops painted him out to be, not at all. No matter what happened in the pen, Vince's business on the outside of the wall continued, just as if Vince was still out on the streets.

Vince's partner Sammy had just gotten out of prison a few months before Vince got locked up. So the ball was now in Sammy and Tony's court to hold Vince's empire down. Mona was now a freshman in high school and her sister Kai was a senior. Mona and the Clique maintained good grades at school and still managed to get work done every Thursday as usual. Nothing changed until one day Lady didn't call or come home. Lady had taken some time out to see her mother-in-law so she could talk to her about some important issues, and make some arrangements she thought she would never have to make. "I can't believe it's come down to this. I'm afraid for my daughters. It's going to be hard telling them what I'm going through," Lady expressed the pain she was feeling as she lay on her mother-in-law's couch, filling out her paperwork.

"I know my daughter; everything will be okay. You just be strong and hang on for as long as you can. I will always love you and be there for you and my grandchildren forever and ever," Frankie's mother replied sitting in her rocking chair telling her daughter-in-law how much she loved her.

Mona and her sisters sat at home and waited for hours until the phone rang. "Hello," Kai answered anxiously.

"Hi baby, it's your Grandma," Gram responded speaking with a soft voice.

"Hi Grams," Kai replied as she lowered her voice as well. "Have you seen my mother today? We haven't seen her all day. She didn't call or come home yet."

Gram answered "Yes baby, your Mommy is fine. She just needed some time to think about a few things and make some important arrangements that's all."

"Well, where is she? And when is she coming home?" Kai shouted. "And Why didn't she let us know where she was?"

"Calm down Kai, your mother needed to talk to me and decided to relax for a moment. Now we will be right over to let you all know what's going on you hear." Gram shouted as she put on her red lipstick.

"Okay," Kai whispered. As Kai hung up the phone, tears rolled down her cheeks. See, Kai already knew what was happening because her mother confided in her and needed her help a while back, since she was her oldest daughter. Kai didn't think that her mother would be telling her sisters what was wrong with her so soon.

It really bothered her because she didn't want her sisters hurting like she was at that moment. When Gram and Lady came home, there was a weird silence in the room.

No one spoke for a few minutes. When their grandmother came from the kitchen, she had a tray of cold drinks for everyone. "Well." Gram muttered "The reason why I'm here with your Mommy is because she needed me to explain something very important to you. Your mother is not well."

"What do you mean not well?" Mia asked. "My mother is sitting right next to you, she's fine."

Gram replied "Yes Mia, she is fine right now but soon she will not be because your Mom is very sick. Your Mom has been sick for quite some time now. She has tried to keep it together but now she is not feeling well."

"Well what is wrong with you Mommy?" Mona asked her mother with great concern in her voice. Lady looked at her daughter and didn't answer her. She couldn't believe she had to explain something so devastating that would change their lives forever.

Their grandmother finally broke the silence and said "Your mother has HIV and she doesn't have much time left to live. Now all of you girls have got to stay strong and look out for one another and help your Mommy when she needs you. Okay?" The news that Gram just delivered felt like a big blow to the heart. No one in the house responded with words. Mona just stared into the air crying silently, while Mia just couldn't help herself running into her mother's arms and holding her tightly with all of her might.

Where did I go wrong? Mona kept thinking to herself over and over again, asking the Lord why does He want their mother to leave them. Mona couldn't quite understand her emotions at the present moment. She didn't know whether to be angry or sad.

All she wanted was for someone to tell her and her sisters that everything will be alright; but that day never arrived. Mona began blaming herself for all the pain that her and her sisters shared. Something inside of her just took over her emotions, leaving her cold as ice. Thinking of all the times she shared with her mom wishing this all was a bad dream. Mona then thought back to the time when her mother took her to a park out in Rosedale Queens for a picnic, just the two of them with her mom asking her what she wanted to do with her life. She told her that she was a bright young lady and could do anything her heart desired. That thought stuck with Mona as she cried silently. When you're young, you don't want to understand hardship. It's just so hard to see your mother at her weakest point. The person who gave you life and brought you into this world. No matter what drug you take, what drink you consume or cigarette you smoke; from liquor to angel dust it's all an escape. And Everyone makes mistakes. Mona couldn't understand that. All the love Mona had in her heart turned into anger and fear.

She wondered why did drugs take her mother and father to a place they didn't know. A place that destroyed their insides and wellbeing. Those thoughts were buried into Mona's head so deep that she too wanted to feel the pain that her precious parents felt.

The thing that fucked Mona's head up the most, was that her mom had been clean for over 12 years and worked five days a week at a nine to five job for 10 years straight. There's just some shit that you will never fully understand. There's some mothers out there who stay fucked up, treating their kids fucked up, getting high 24/7, prostituting their bodies for a quick fix, not giving a fuck about their children or grandchildren, but they're alive and kicking it like it ain't nothing. God certainly picks his angels for a reason. And Mother is most certainly one of them. A guardian angel chosen to fly home to a much better place where there is no pain or suffering. After hearing the bad news, Mona's whole frame of thought changed. She became very depressed and lost her way. Mona stayed to herself a lot. She would stay in her room everyday writing in a notepad her mom brought her. She had so many bottled up feelings and emotions and didn't quite know how to express herself with words through speech, so Mona continued to write. Everything drastically changed with Mona.

Her heart grew so heavy filled with pain and disbelief. She started hanging out with the wrong chicks, sniffing cocaine and drinking. Central bookings became Mona's second home due to fighting and boosting out of high end stores. So much damage can be done when running away from your problems.

There were more than rough days in Mona's calendar. And lessons were surely learned through each experience. God surely was on Mona's side through the tests of time especially with Mona still blessed with her natural beauty. One gloomy day Mona made eye contact with a Judge who said the next time he saw her she would spend a few years in prison. Mona woke up quick!

HOOD GAMES

After many cloudy days, Lady and her girls shared a lot of good times together as well. They did everything big. Christmas shopping sprees, picnics, BBQ's and family dinners at their grandmother's house on their mother side, enjoying each other and creating sweet memories.

Lady began living on the first floor of her mother's house. She looked exactly like her mother who was short and sweet and didn't speak a lick of English. Lady's mother was from Ponce Puerto Rico, where Lady and her siblings were born and raised as children, until their mom and dad moved to Jamaica Queens NY. Abuela cooked Spanish meals for her entire family. She served the best tasting Spanish dishes in the world, at exactly 12pm sharp.

She had a weekly menu filled with a different dish for each day. The best days out of the week were Tuesday's, when she cooked beef stew, white rice and plantains and on Saturday's when she made chicken, beef or mondongo/tripe soup with domplinas and pasteles on the side. Her food was delicious! There's nothing better than the smell of your grandmother's home cooking, God bless her soul. Just when people begin to smile and make things right; there's always something lurking around ready to knock things right back down again. Things started getting rough with Lady's well-being. And the nightmare had just begun.

Just the thought of losing a loved one could be devastating to a child or anyone for that matter. Especially if that loved one is your mother. You only get one mother! Until you too are forced to witness this same experience; then you will understand this feeling. It's like a whole in your heart that could never be sealed.

Even if you do witness the same loss, there is no telling how you may react.

Every human being has a different way of dealing with their emotions. And the thought of losing Lady, made Mona very angry. To bear witness of a loved one becoming ill and watching them lose control of their health and life is an extremely hard experience to endure. Sometimes the toughest things in life can make you the strongest. It's either you suffer in sadness, dwelling on the past and misfortunes, or you pick yourself up out of a bad situation, wiping your tears and visualize the problem at hand. There is no quick way to ease trauma and pain, but there is a way to cope in every situation. Mona couldn't pinpoint what direction she was going through all the clouds before her, but she surely knew that she would make her mother proud once she reached her destination.

Mona told her Mom how much she loved her, but never got the chance to show her how much she's grown as a young lady and share her hopes and dreams. Sometimes you think you have all the time in the world to let someone know how much they mean to you when time is running against you ticking away at its wit. *"If only I could talk to her one last time and tell her she's the best thing that ever happened to me."* Mona thought as her mother slept in her bedroom. Hug and share with your loved ones and tell them how you feel. Share your heart and be the hand that they can hold on to. For it may be the last time you'll ever see them! *Love You Mother...*

MONA

CHAPTER
Nine

"You don't have to think that way Mona," Tony mentioned as he stared at Mona with a look of concern on his face. "Don't you ever wonder if the family is worried about you?" He asked while he rolled his blunt. "I can't stand to see you like this sis, we stronger than that remember." Tony whispered as he looked down at Mona sitting on the seal in the park.

"Yeah I know!" Mona answered, sniffing on some powder and chasing it with a shot of Hennessy.

Mona looked up at her best friend Tony with admiration. Her big light brown eyes admired him for caring so much. Mona hadn't been home in weeks and although she appeared beautiful physically, her mind and spirit was weak mentally. Mona wanted to be home with her mom and sisters more than life itself, but she chose to stay away. In the meantime, Lady was worried about her daughter who was living in the streets while her illness took a turn for the worse.

Mona was beautiful. She wore a tan mink jacket with a short gray dress and high heeled stilettos. Her hair was very long, streaming down her back. Mona's light brown eyes complimented her light skinned complexion. She was in pain, sniffing cocaine and drinking to numb her feelings and emotions. Mona didn't want to hurt her family at all.

All Mona wanted was for someone to understand her. Deep down inside she was hurting tremendously. She was so afraid of reality that running away from her problems and partying just took over her mind. The streets were the only thing she loved at that moment. What is a girl to do when she's lost the only man who ever truly loved her and then lost her innocence to someone she thought she could trust. Not only did it make Mona promiscuous, but it also made her rebellious and very angry. She had trust issues with men and she stayed away from loving relationships. She was searching for her purpose in life. To find it, she had to stumble over many obstacles. Sometimes the only way to move forward is to revisit the things in your past that are holding you back. You have to deal with them head on no matter how scary they may be. Once you do, you'll see that you can go further than you imagined. Some people can't cope with trauma or abuse and they find many ways to escape their fears and darkness. That's when a wall gets built and trust issues appear. Although Mona was struggling with her demons, she was also challenging her inner strengths. Mona's friend Tony didn't know about her childhood struggles and that's why he found himself constantly questioning her ways.

Now that her mother was sick, it just made everything ten times worse. Mona's style was very unique and she knew it. She had the body of a model and the face of a goddess. But her pain didn't match her persona. Partying and drinking became a known hobby of hers. Mona was a child when she was introduced into the drug game and she'd been bagging up drugs for so long that it seemed like normal behavior for her. Mona's lifestyle was way different than your average teenager. Although she lived a rough lifestyle, she carried herself very well and remained beautiful like a princess.

91

"Is drug addiction and alcoholism hereditary?" Mona asked Tony as she licked her lips while putting on her lip gloss. Mona smiled at the mirror she pulled out of her purse as she waited for Tony to answer her.

Tony just puffed on his blunt saying "I don't know, shit. If it is, you damn sure caught it," laughing as he held Mona, letting her know that he was only joking. Mona just stared at Tony with her big brown eyes smiling right back. Mona and Tony would talk to one another for hours just to keep each other on point. They shared a real bond and friendship and had each other's back no matter what. There weren't many people who knew how to make Mona smile. Tony just had the magic touch. Mona stayed up in the hottest clubs and bars making major moves meeting new people and becoming very much involved with music.

Music had always been her first love. She'd sing at talent shows and open mic nights, meeting with new artists that were coming out and getting plenty exposure. She practically knew everybody who could sing or rap from Queens, N.Y. Either they went to her school, came from the same projects or met up at an industry party. Not to mention that Tony knew a lot of entertainers also and he would introduce Mona to everyone. Listening to old school slow jams back at home as a youngster left a big impact on Mona growing up. She was very aware of all kinds of music, old and new. Her voice was beautiful. She sang like a songbird. Young lady, had soul running through her veins from jump.

Writing songs and stories was a way to release the many stresses in her life and a way she coped with pain. Writing was her way to meditate.

Every time Mona picked up a pen, it felt like she was fighting her biggest fears. Mona could give a fuck about what anyone thought because no one lived in her shoes and what really mattered was how she truly felt deep within.

There was going to be a major party for "NAS!.' This rapper from Queens was the hottest thing out. Everyone in the hood was really hyped about it. Mona had made it her business to call her sister Kai to see what was up with their Mom and ask if Kai and the Clique was going to the jump off.

Mona's mother and sisters were very happy to hear from her and made Mona aware of how important she was to the family and that they must stick together to get through all battles and hardships no matter what. Mona took heed to what had been said and listened to her family. She made plans to move back home really soon. Smiling from ear-to-ear, happy that she had gotten up enough nerve to place a quarter in the phone and call home, Mona was pleased with herself and planned on having a great night.

The club scene was jumping inside and out. It was that 90's Era. There were celebrities and stars everywhere. A big-time playa from around the way was making announcements as the DJ was spinning on the turn tables. 'Nas- 'Illmatic' was all you heard playing in the club people were happy and content, singing along with the songs, dancing and smiling just having a ball. Tony and the girls were all on point in VIP where all the playas were. Looking at her watch, Kai began to wonder where Mona was and what was keeping her.

Meanwhile, Mona was stuck outside the club due to the lack of ID. Mona had purchased a fake driver's license one winter for a couple hundred dollars when she and the Clique went to Mardi Gras out in New Orleans. Looking for her license on the line, Mona had remembered that she left her ID in her other purse over at her boyfriend's crib.

Everybody that knew Mona, who had some juice, was already inside the club getting their groove on. Mona decided to catch a cab to her boyfriend's house, get her license and return so she can enter the club. While hailing a cab, Mona saw two guys whom she knew from the hood. The guys she saw stopped to talk to her for a minute about the likings of the club when Mona explained to them how she didn't have her license and couldn't get inside the club without it. Tank' offered Mona a ride to go and retrieve her ID and bring her back to the club, since he was going also but had to make a quick run elsewhere. Mona agreed and entered the car. Once inside, drinks were being poured and music was blasting. Mona had also smelled a strong marijuana blunt laced with coke.

"You alright? You need a drink to hold you down until we get back to the club?" Tank asked sarcastically as he drove the car.

Mona answered, "Yeah, no doubt Tank." Tank was a known hustler in the hood who silently had a vendetta against Vince and his goons. He always been jealous of the relationship that Vince and Tony shared and held a grudge behind it. As far as Mona knew, Tank was just another dude that kissed ass, trying to get like Vince.

She had no idea of his intentions. Even though Vince was in the pen, Tank still wanted to see someone whom he loved dearly hurt, or even worse for that matter since Vince never fucked with him or gave a play to any of his connects. Mona just happened to be the bait.

This goes to show you that you never really know what a person's intentions are when they are around you. People will smile in your face and think of killing you at the same time. Mona thanked Tank for the Hennessy and without a second thought she guzzled it down with no chaser whatsoever. "Damn Mona, you better be careful with that," Tank responded smiling while looking through the rear-view mirror.

"Don't worry I know how to handle my liquor Tank," Mona replied. "You just watch the road and worry about us getting back to the club so we can all have a good time once I meet up with my Clique," she continued, wiping the Hennessy from the side of her mouth.

"Hey Tank, looks like we got ourselves a live one here. And it looks like she needs another shot," Tank's friend interrupted sitting in the back seat with Mona. Looking into the rearview, Tank signaled his friend to pour Mona another shot of Hennessy. This time Mona's drink had been laced with drugs. They gave her Liquid X, a dangerous substance that comes in a liquid or powder form. Consuming it can cause dizziness, unconsciousness or coma.

Most people have no idea they are being drugged and become victim to predators who prey on women for sexual pleasure.

Mona began explaining to the driver that he had driven too far and needed to make a U-turn back towards her boyfriend's crib. Tank ignored Mona's request and kept driving in the opposite direction. By this time, the drink that she was offered had been sipped slowly until all of the contents in the cup was gone. Tank's friend then told Mona to relax while he forcefully placed his hand up her thigh.

Mona could feel that something was wrong because her eye-lids became very heavy. Looking around, Mona could see nothing but a blur. The music in the car became extremely loud and just thumped in the back of her head. Before she knew what had happened, Mona was laid out in the back seat with her eyes closed.

Kizz and Kai sat over in VIP with Niema and Tony while Kema flew to the dance floor when she heard her song playing. Sierra didn't enter the club because she had bumped into her man outside and they wound up getting into a big fight and going home before she even stepped inside.

"There's no telling what happened with Mona," Kai sighed. "I'm going to see if she left me any messages," she said, as she walked towards the restroom to check her cell phone. While checking her phone, Kai heard a message from Mona stating that she was on her way to the club about 2 hours ago. But she hadn't seen her sister yet. Kai then checked her two way pager to see if her sister left her a text. There were no new pages or texts listed. By this time everyone in the crew was worried and insisted on looking around the club to see if they saw her. There was no sign of Mona anywhere!

The next morning, Mona had awakened from a deep sleep in the back of an abandoned car. Her hair was still in place but her face was bruised. Her clothes were thrown all over the front seat of the car, and her purse and shoes were found outside. Crying softly, Mona reached down to feel her vagina and it felt really sore and swollen. Dressing her naked body, Mona reached inside of her purse for her phone to call her sister for help. Mona could not remember anything. Her memory was blank and she was fighting really hard to remember what happened. The only thing she did remember, was standing in front of the club talking to Tank and his friend and being offered a ride to retrieve her ID.

That thought flashed before Mona's eyes over a dozen times before speaking to her sister. While the phone rang, Mona's hands shook nervously as she awaited an answer. Kai's phone didn't pick up so Mona decided on calling Tony. The tears that burst out of Mona's eyes hardly helped her to dial Tony's number so she gently wiped her face with a tissue. "Hello" Mona said crying softly. "Hello, Tony?"

Tony answered "Where the fuck are you Mona? What's wrong sis?"

"I've been raped Tony and I really need you to come get me," she told him with tears running down her face.

"What?! What did you say Mona," Tony asked not wanting to believe what he'd thought he heard.

Mona started crying so loud that Tony could hardly understand her. Mona shouted "I've been raped Tony and I really need you to come get me please."

Tony couldn't believe what he was hearing, he jumped out of bed waking the whole house hollering, "I'm gonna kill them motherfuckers! I'm on my way Mona!" Kai, Tony and the girls stayed at Niema's apartment that night to avoid unnecessary driving since everyone was fucked up last night. Kai told her mom that they all were together to avoid her from worrying over her and Mona.

"What's wrong Tony? Where are you going?" Niema asked washing her face off with a washcloth.

"I'm going to get Mona. She's hurt and she needs me." When Tony slammed the door behind him, the girls realized what Tony had said and within seconds they were right behind him jumping into his ride. Tony had stayed on the phone with Mona until he reached her. While waiting at the light, Tony's other line beeped on his phone so he answered. On the other end of the line was one of Tony's goons telling him how Tank and his man had been bragging about raping Mona last night. By this time Tony had fire in his eyes and his cell phone dropped to the floor.

Niema kept asking "What's wrong? Is Mona alright?"

Tony answered Niema, saying just one name, Tony said "It was Tank!" as he cocked his gun and placed it on safety. Tony put the gun by his side and drove at full speed to find his best friend. When they finally reached Mona, she was leaning on the car crying.

The Clique held Mona and kissed her over and over. Tony whispered to Mona and said "Everything will be okay and I'm going to get the bastard that violated you. But first we need to take you to the hospital."

Mona was afraid of going to the hospital because she didn't want them to notify the police about her rape and plus she was really embarrassed. The Clique insisted that she'd go just to see if everything was ok with her. Tony dropped the girls off at the emergency room and then sped off in his truck, burning his tires on the street.

At the hospital, Mona was visited by a rape victim specialist and was given a rape kit test. She was also comforted by the nurse on staff. She was given a choice in as to whether she wanted to keep the rape confidential or report it to the police. The nurse then explained to Mona that there was a small amount of semen found on her private area. The evidence was still present because Mona hadn't showered before she visited the hospital. Mona felt better knowing that there would be evidence against her rapist if she decided to press charges. But at the same time, Mona wanted to stay true to the code of the streets and handle Tank by any means. Then she thought about Tony and already knew he was headed straight into Tank's direction. With the girls by her side, Mona decided to press charges at a later time. All Mona wanted to do was go home to see her mom, take a shower and relax.

Being back home was very soothing for Mona. Although she cried for a few days, she regained her inner strength. She was happy to be close with her family again. Mona told her mother about the rape because she knew she did nothing wrong. She also let her mother know that the streets were going to get the motherfucker that attacked her.

Having little memory of the attack really helped Mona to move forward quickly and positively. Mona remained home and helped her sisters care for their ill mother. Their mother was very dependent on her daughters and needed help from all three of her children.

Mona woke up in good spirits ironing her denim jeans, listening to music, when her phone rang. "Hello," Mona answered. "Mona what's up sis? Get dressed I'm coming to get you. Be ready in one hour." Tony replied hanging up the phone. Tony met up with Mona one sunny afternoon and took her too 'Tony Roma's' on Queens Blvd. They talked for hours laughing and joking over steak and shrimp, it was a really good day. Tony and Mona began to talk about how she's been feeling. When Mona spoke saying, "Tony I really don't want you to retaliate against Tank. That punk is going to get his, mark my words." "Every dog has their day!"

Mona saw blood every time she thought about Tank but she just didn't want her friend Tony catching a murder and getting caught up over a thirsty motherfucker. Tony didn't get to kill Tank like he wanted to because Tank was already caught up in a world of his own troubles. "Well Mona it's funny you said that, because the motherfucker in jail without bail as we speak.!" Tony mentioned while he chewed on his steak. Mona just stared at Tony sipping on her Romarita.

Tank remained low key, still hustling and selling dope near South road with the same sarcastic, fuck you attitude. Although Mona never pressed charges on Tank; he wound up raping another chick, then he caught a slew of gun and drug charges which sent him off to prison for a very long time.

When he got locked up, he became the girlfriend of a big dude named Bubba, getting his salad tossed every night. Bubba found the man of his dreams and made Tank his little bitch, setting that ass straight. "God sure don't like ugly!" Tony smirked telling Mona about Tank. They both looked at each other and laughed as they enjoyed their meal...

TONY

CHAPTER
Ten

"Damn man, shit!" Tony roared. "I done told you before about coming up short with my fucking money. I go through this shit with your ass every fucking week," Tony shouted, looking down at his diamond imbedded watch. "Listen! If you don't come up with my money by 6pm tonight. My gun is going to blow smoke straight up your ass. You understand?" Tony asked, back smacking the dude and hitting him with his pinky ring.

"Yeah Tony I understand I'll have your bread, I'll get your money," Benny cried holding his face. There was absolutely nothing left to discuss. Benny just stood there silent, bloody faced and still sprawled out against the car as if someone was still holding him. He stayed in that position until Tony sped off in his truck.

Dope and coke was the top selling drugs out and Tony had all the inside connects from Queens to Jersey. Meeting up with the Columbians in abandoned buildings was the hardest part of the game. Not that Tony was afraid of the Columbians who sold him kilos of coke. He just never felt too comfortable around them while conducting business.

You could never be too sure of what might happen when you're buying a large quantity of drugs in an abandoned building where there is no one else in sight but you, your partner you came with, and about ten fucking Columbians inside one huge apartment.

Tony felt he was taking a chance each and every time he made a trip Uptown to re-up, but hey, somebody had to do it. Tony's connections were inherited through his main boss Vince. Vince was like a father to Tony and taught him everything he knew. Now that Vince is serving life in prison, Tony had become the new king of the hood and had an empire big enough to feed everybody in it. Tony was brown skinned and very handsome. His style was simple and fresh! Tony wore a fresh pair of Timberlands, dark blue denim jeans with a Pelle Pelle leather jacket.

He had a real short temper when it came to his money. Tony had a great personality but was quick to peel a few caps back at the drop of a dime. Although everything was all good in the streets, Tony kept up his monthly visits to see Vince. He even sent a few chicks to the pen every now and then with a couple balloons so Vince could set up shop and have shit on lock while he was on the inside. Just because Vince was locked up, didn't mean his life was at a complete halt! Vince married his main chick, got pussy on the regular, stayed with major paper and even cooked his own meals while he was Upstate.

Vince became especially close to one of the Correctional Officers so they would have his back whenever he sold his drugs and cigarettes in the pen to all of the inmates.

Of course, the CO's managed to get a piece of his profit and Vince had the prison on lock. Vince's goons started following Tony's orders and Tony looked up to Vince's partner Sammy for everything else. Shit was still the same, except for the fact that Vince wasn't in the streets. Other than that, the ball just kept rolling in the dough. Tony was chilling down the hill with the Clique, cracking up on old times, drinking Moet and smoking trees when he looked at his watch and saw that it was 7:45 pm. Tony then thought about Benny and was ready to make good on his threat.

Benny usually gave Tony $2000 after every shift and he worked 4 days out of the week. This week, Benny's been coming up $400 short every day and now he owes Tony $1600. Tony would let a motherfucker slide if he says he had to take care of something or needed the money for a reason. But Benny thought he could do whatever he wanted without a consequence and he was clearly mistaken. Tony sent one of his boys to walk around the projects to see if he saw the little motherfucker. There was no sign of Benny anywhere.

The look on Tony's face had made shit very obvious that he wanted to kill him. Instead of expressing his anger, Tony remained cool and continued the conversation he was having with his girls. Tony loved chilling out with the Clique because they were his family and were the only people who made him feel comfortable, like he was at home, no matter what! They all had gotten extremely close since the passing of Mona's mom. The girls had taken their mother's death really hard and for a minute shit had gotten real bitter with their family.

It happens with every death! A bunch of family drama, a bunch of *'who's getting what, who did what, who wants what and who ain't getting shit'*. Mona's mom had become very ill and she told her daughters that she didn't want to stay in the hospital at all. Lady wanted to come home where she was comfortable with her family and that's exactly where she stayed. Mona had awakened one gloomy morning at home and made her way into the kitchen to get some orange juice.   On the way back to her room, she had checked on her Mom to see how she was feeling that day.

Entering the room, Mona looked at her mother and she was gone. Her mother was no longer. Lady passed away that dreadful morning at her home, resting in peace. Tears ran down Mona's cheeks as she began to scream dropping her cup of juice and running for the comfort of her sister Kai. That was the toughest day of their lives. Learning that your mother passed away is hard enough as is. But for Mona to find her mother dead like that was very overwhelming.

"Kai, I can't believe all the drama that's going on right now. Our mother is not even buried yet and the only thing this mother fucker thinking about is selling grandma's house. Nobody came to see or help mommy while she was sick. It feels like they were just waiting for her to pass away." Mona spoke to her sister as she curled her hair in the bathroom. Mona was very emotional one morning after coming home and seeing a for sale sign on their grandmother's house the same week their mother was in the morgue. The same house their grandmother lived in for over 40yrs raising all her children and grands. The same house their grandmother still resided in was being swept beneath her feet by her own daughter.

Their aunt Leola didn't care about anyone but herself. Leola held a grudge against her sister's daughter Mona for accusing her son Waynie of molesting her. She blatantly told Mona that she never wanted to get to know her after her mom passed away. Her actions were spiteful and her intentions were very cruel. She didn't give a damn about the family house, the memories, or the love. She just saw dollar signs. Leola was on a mission and she was willing to destroy anyone who got in her way. She was a mean, cold hearted, evil witch. "Mona don't even sweat it, this too shall pass. We have to stick together as sisters and be there for each other like we were there for our mother. There is going to be a lot of rough times ahead of us and right now, my only concern is me, you and Mia!" Kai muttered as she prepared for their mother's funeral. A lot of family drama and issues erupted after Lady passed away. There were so many open wounds and unclosed issues stabbing at the heart. The one thing that remained sweet through all the drama was the unbreakable bond between three sisters who had witnessed the unbearable and survived through it all still standing and loving each other and God is surely good for that. There will always be problems with family, but at the end of the day, you can't pick and choose your family. Everyone has issues in life and sometimes you have to outweigh the good from the bad and keep it moving.

Without love and understanding, you will never be able to overcome and rejoice. It's either you let go, let god and work through certain differences or just move the fuck on! Mona and her sisters bond became tight as ever. As well as Mona and Tony's. They were like Bonnie and Clyde. Wherever you saw Tony, Mona followed. She even carried her own silver 22 inside of her purse in case anything ever popped off.

Since Tony had no clue as to where to find Benny, his guard stayed up because he didn't know what ideas Benny was planning in his head. Plus, Benny had never acted this way before. Whenever Tony told one of his goons to do something it was done. Benny's actions were far from normal. A few weeks had passed and the club scene was off the hook, Grey door, Q Club and Joe's after hour spot; all that hot shit just kept the party jumping and then some. The Clique was faithfully holding shit down for Tony who had the hood on lock and up under his wing. Benny had been replaced since he disappeared after getting his ass kicked and his face hadn't been seen since Tone bruised it.

Tony was sitting in his truck down the hill in the projects. He came to pick up a few bundles from Kai and Mona. "What's up Tony?" Kai smiled closing the back door of Tony's truck. What up sis, Tony replied sitting in the driver seat. Mona opened Tony's truck and shouted "Tony let me tell you what I just heard about this motherfucker Benny," slamming his front door when she climbed in. Tony looked at Mona with the side eye wondering what she heard about Benny. Mona continued "Word out on the streets is that Benny has been seen numerous times with that chick Sasha's uncle Lem. He also been running off at the mouth telling him unnecessary information." Mona spoke looking into Tony's face. "Yo! this mother fucker needs to get his ass whipped." Kai snarled popping her gum. "Oh word!" Tony responded! "This bitch ass nigga switching gears and holding grudges when he was in the wrong to begin with, taking money that wasn't his to claim. If he would've asked for the money, shit would be smooth like butter. But he didn't, so he got dealt with." "He better have a lot of fucking heat on him when I catch his ass, that motherfucker is dead."

Tony shouted with his gun in his hand. The news that he just heard set him on a whole new level of violence once he saw Benny. "Oh this nigga rather go against me, then to be loyal on the same team. He's biting the hand that's been feeding him since day one." Tony was on fire but he held his composure until he found out some more details of what's really going on.

There had been over two dozen robberies lately in the projects and throughout the hood. A couple of crews were shook up too, but Tony wasn't too concerned with the gossip because he had a pretty good idea of what was going down.

Tony knew a lot of stick up kids too. Some were from the hood and some were in the rap game. Every now and then Tony, Mona and the Clique received a few hot pieces here and there to keep that ball rolling. A lot of hot games were played in the hood and the goons who played them were most definitely paid for their troubles. Tony paid these guys good paper just on the strength of the struggle. Everyday life is a hustle and Tony knocked no one for what they did to survive. It may not be today, but sooner or later you will have to get up off your ass and find a way to make that paper stack! Life is too short to be sitting at home twiddling your thumbs wondering when your next meal is going to be. Yeah Ok! You gotta step into this game, make that money and get in where you fit in or stay the fuck out of the way and Tony did just that by any means. One thing Tony didn't respect was a fake bitch ass nigga!

Sitting in a truck with tinted windows with Sasha's uncle Lem. Benny shouted, "Yeah this motherfucker done beat your niece then left her with his goons.

108

After Vince bounced, these goons really had their way with this girl. Then they dressed her up and fed her to the sharks near West Side Highway, where she became fresh meat for the pimps and hoes. She was lucky though, because she could've been shot and left for dead bleeding like a wounded animal." Benny explained the events of Sasha's beat down which led her to the track. Telling Lem that he believes til this day that Sasha was used as an example in case anyone else ever felt the urge to cross Vince. Benny then shouted "Now you gonna let them motherfuckers shit on your niece like that or are you gonna bring it like a real nigga should, huh?" Benny just brought the beast out of Sasha's uncle Lem. Lem didn't see nothing else but Sasha screaming in his eyes and he was filled with vengeance.

Actually, Benny didn't have a clue as to what he just done. Thinking he was getting back at Tony by snitching on Vince's goons when he too was there having his way with Sasha. Lem began wondering in his hot head about how Benny knew of all this info and never thought of telling him before. Asking himself *"How could this bitch ass nigga look me in my face every fucking day handle his business and not tell me shit. If Tony didn't kick his ass, he would have never told me that shit."* Coming back from his hurt and angry world, Lem just stood there silently listening to all the bullshit Benny was talking and then Lem finally said "Ayo, let's go get some liquor Benny because I need a drink my man."

"I can't believe those bastards did my niece like that," Lem muttered with his hands on his forehead. "What could she have done to make these dudes go off on her like that?"

"I don't know Lem," Benny answered "This is news to me too. As soon as I found out who did that shit to Sasha I couldn't wait to get at you to tell you because you my man." Both Lem and Benny hopped onto the highway and headed towards the Triborough Bridge. Once they reached Harlem, Benny copped some weed from 145th street after Lem had picked up some Hennessy from the liquor store.

Lem then got a call from one of his cousins who was chilling at the after-hour spot on St. Nicholas. Lem's cousin told him to make sure his pockets were right because they were gambling and shit. Everything was smooth and Lem had planned everything out in his mind what he needed to do for his niece Sasha. When Lem pulled up on St. Nicholas, he called his cousin Reese and told him to meet him and Benny outside before they entered the spot. Lem gave his cousin a brief rundown about everything that happened and they both were in agreement to his decisions.

Lem began counting his money, handed Reese a pound and then took a few pulls off the blunt Benny rolled. Once inside the spot, the fellas were greeted and offered drinks, coke and a host of other shit! There were a few hoes, walking around in practically nothing, serving hot wings, crab legs and cakes, fried fish with chips and a side of pussy! The food was slamming and there were piles of money on top of the pool table where the fellas gambled and Lem wanted in. Everything was going as planned. Everybody was fucked up losing to one another, arguing back and forth about who rolled what and who pays who.

Benny was sitting in the cut, kicking it to one of the chicks serving food when all of a sudden Reese decided to tap his bottle to make a toast. Everyone stood still for a moment then gathered around by the pool table where everybody gambled. Reese shouted "It's been a good year. We made some money, fucked some good pussy, you know shit been real. But just when you think you about to have yourself a good night; something always comes and hit you right in the face."

No one in the room understood anything Reese was trying to say. Lem interrupted saying, "Yeah this is a special shout out to my man Benny." Everyone held their glasses in the air ready to toast so they could continue on with their evening.

Reese cleared his throat to get everyone's attention again. Then he said "Good looking Benny, this is for Sasha." When Benny lifted his glass up to Reese, Lem pulled out his gun and shot Benny in the head. Blood splattered all over the girl serving crab cakes. Glasses flying out of hands from people dropping their drinks and bottles of champagne on the floor.

People started running in every direction trying to get to the outside of the spot. Benny's brains were on the wall and his body was slumped over top of the pool table leaving everyone's money stained with blood. "Ayo', Lem, let's go," Reese shouted. "Lem, we gotta get the fuck out of here, come on." No matter how loud Reese screamed at his cousin, Lem could not hear his voice. He just stood there blank faced with his gun still drawn staring at Benny watching him bleed to death. "Man, fuck this shit I'm out of here," Reese screamed as he headed for the door.

Lem awakened from his rage running over to the pool table stuffing piles of bloody money into his pockets and then followed his cousin who was already headed towards his truck. Lem handed Reese his keys and then hopped into the passenger seat as they both drove back across the Bridge to Queens in full speed. "Damn!" Reese yelled leery eyed. I can't believe I let you talk me into this shit man. When I called your monkey ass on the phone I was expecting a good mother fuckin night, making some money and getting fucked up. Now I'm sitting here with a murder under my belt.

Lem shouted "Yo, shut the fuck up and drive Reese. All that shit is the least of my worries. That bitch Benny is just the beginning of this shit here. You better believe I'm gonna catch every last one of them mother fuckers who fucked with my niece."

     *   *   *   *   *   *

Tony was enjoying some much needed rest laid up at home with his girl who was gazing at the television; when he was awakened by the telephone ringing at 8am in the morning.

Still sleeping, Tony answered the phone. "This is a collect call from Clinton Correctional Facility. To accept please press 3 now!" "Hello!" Tony answered. Vince replied "Yeah Tony morning." Tony whispered 'Morning Vince." 'How is everybody?" Vince asked. "Oh, everybody's good," Tony quickly answered and yourself. Vince said, "Oh I'm holding it down. "Listen!" "Have you seen all of your boys from downtown?" Vince asked with concern in his voice. "I'm hearing a couple Katz got killed up in Harlem put me on." "What you mean Vince?"

"I've been chilling taking it easy for a few days just to keep shit tight. Everything was clean out in the streets last I saw." Tony responded surprised. Vince replied "Well I'm hearing different. This motherfucker Lem is on some vendetta shit against the family and he's talking a lot of shit out there that's all. Tony just be on point out there and watch these motherfuckers around you-you hear. Everybody ain't down with the same team." Vince spoke firmly! Tony replied "I hear you Vince, I'm straight now, thanks for calling one love." Hanging up the phone, Tony was now wide awake scrambling his shirt over his head.

Tony shouted "Get dressed baby we leaving." "Is Everything alright?" Tony's girl answered worried. "Everything is fine baby I'm just taking you home that's all.

Something came up and I need to handle some business." Tony whispered to his girl beside him while running his fingers through her hair. Tony then told her he was driving her car for the day. "You take my truck and go buy yourself something pretty okay." Handing his girl a wad of cash and smacking her on the ass as he sent her to shower. While Laurie showered, Tony made his way down to his truck to switch all of his belongings to Laurie's car.

Tony took his gun and money that he kept inside of a secret compartment. Then took his Timbs and clothes out of the trunk and placed them into the car. After following Laurie home, Tony drove to the projects to find out about what went down a couple nights ago. Tony had been blind to everything around him for the past few days. Due to the fact that when he's alone spending quality time with his girl; he feels like he's on cloud 9 in a class all by himself. He also has a habit of turning off all outside distractions until he's ready to attend to them.

He knew something was up when Mona and Kai told him that shit about Benny, but he had no idea that shit was that serious. Now this kind of thinking can be pleasurable from time to time. Everyone needs time to relax. It also can be a very huge mistake on his part. You never know when situations like this will take place living in the fast life. Shit was definitely real in the streets and there was a problem at hand that needed to be ceased immediately. Tony knew in his mind that this shit with Sasha would come up one way or another; but never in his wildest dreams did he think that one of his goons would cross him and Vince the way Benny just did. *"All this shit here is a product of Vince's anger over Sasha's sticky fingers."*

As Tony drove through Jamaica Queens, he thought to himself as he switched through the lanes on the Van Wyck. *"That bitch should've never fucked with Vince. She lucky to be alive today."* Sitting up at 'Carmichael's Diner' in Baisley Projects, the gentleman placed his order.

113

"Yes, I'll have fried fish and grits with cheese." Sammy spoke to the waitress before him. "Would you like some orange juice with that Sir?" The young waitress asked as Sammy answered "Yes large please."

Then Tony interrupted and shouted "Make that two orders please." Tony sat down for breakfast with one of Vince's oldest partners in the game. Sammy was one of the most ruthless drug lords from Spanish Harlem who linked up with Vince when he first started out in the early 80's. Sammy had given Tony some input on the possible whereabouts of Lem and his cousin Reese. "Listen Tony these motherfuckers are on a warpath and they are coming for you. You need to be on point and on the lookout 24/7 it's not a fucking game." Sammy continued "Lem viciously shot Benny in the head in front of 30 people. He blew his fucking brains out on St. Nicholas three nights ago. This shit is crazy." Tony was in shock when he heard of Benny's murder and how Lem's been looking for him and anyone close to him ever since.

"I wanted to personally inform you of the seriousness of this beef Tony. Lem Must Die Immediately!" Sammy roared as he slammed his orange juice on the table. After breakfast, Sammy had Tony follow him to his crib on the lower eastside of Harlem. Tony had a lot on his plate now that Sammy woke him up from his journey on cloud 9.

"It was either kill or be killed." Tony thought to himself behind the walls of an Upstate Federal Prison.

It's been about a month since Tony's been locked up and he hadn't talked to anyone at home or in the pen. Tony was sentenced to 10yrs in prison with the possibility of parole in five.

"Who'd a thought shit would end up like this huh?" Tony asked Vince in one of many letters that he wrote to him. Tony wrote letters to Vince while he was in the pen and sent them to his girl Laurie to mail to Vince Upstate. Tony wrote "Everything was perfect, with no worries and no mistakes. Where did we go wrong?" Tony asked Vince saying, "I know one thing for sure. I'd rather be up in the pen than to be sitting up in somebody's cemetery. At least I'm able to make decisions and see my people whenever I'm ready to face them. Vince, I just wanted to tell you thanks for being there for me."

"Everything that led me to this point was because of me. I made the choice to choose this life and this is my consequence. Killing Lem was a due or die situation you understand. I had no choice for that matter. That's all my man, see you when I reach Clinton one."

After eating breakfast, both Sammy and Tony broke out to Sammy's crib for a minute. Sammy had purchased some brand new and improved bullet proof vests that he really wanted Tony to try out. Sammy's condo was huge with 4 bedrooms and was laced with fine antique furniture. Entering into the living room, Tony noticed the vests sitting on Sammy's couch. "Yo Sammy, these vests are hot." Tony shouted trying on the bullet proof vest that Sammy just brought for them. "Yeah!" "Who you telling. This that body armor, better safe than sorry nigga." Sammy yelled smiling at Tony. They finally sat down to a few shots of Hennessy. Sammy had also taken a few lines of coke and before you knew it, it was a quarter to 8pm. So Sammy and Tony decided to meet up with everyone at the sports bar out in Midtown. Before leaving the crib, Sammy took off his vest and went to his master bedroom to change into his navy-blue sweater and gators.

Turning the light on, something in the room felt a little strange but Sammy thought nothing of it at the time. Little did he know, Lem had followed Sammy to his condo earlier that morning. Sammy walked over to his walk-in closet and slid the door open.

115

Standing in the closet was Lem with a fully loaded gun aiming directly at Sammy. "If you gonna shoot me motherfucker, shoot me bitch." Sammy snarled staring directly into Lem's eyes. Those were the last words indeed to come out of Sammy's mouth. Lem shot Sammy three times. Hitting him once in the shoulder, and two times in the chest at close range.

Sammy's fatal mistake was taking his vest off when he went to go change his footwear. Still sitting on the couch, Tony heard shots coming from one of Sammy's bedrooms and ran in its direction. Looking from outside, Tony could see Sammy laying helplessly from the hallway. Lem stood over Sammy ready to shoot him again when Tony just rang out shots one after another hitting Lem in the back and gut. Running into the room at the same time, Tony just kept shooting when Reese came out from under the bed shooting Tony in the leg and chest.

All Tony saw was blood in his eyes. When Reese shot Tony, he fell backwards still shooting hitting Reese in the stomach and dick. Everyone was hit and there was no man standing. Tony could hear Reese screaming and hollering from behind the bed. Dragging his body towards the screams, Tony felt his leg burning and gushing with blood. At this point Tony didn't give a fuck he just wanted the screams to stop. Finally, the crib was quiet after Reese took a single shot to the head shutting him up forever. Tony was the only man breathing. He could hear the loud sirens from the streets coming closer towards Sammy's condo.

Busting into the condo, with guns drawn, the police found Tony and the remaining dead bodies in a pool of blood. The police shouted "You have the right to remain silent." When Tony screamed "Yo, can't you see me bleeding motherfucker." The police continued "Anything you say will be held against you in a court of law." The cops cuffed Tony and took him straight to the hospital. Tony suffered a single shot to his right leg.

The shot he took to the chest could've been fatal, but the bullet didn't rip through the vest thanks to Sammy.

Tony pleaded self- defense but had a slew of felony charges. His charges were lessened due to the perps who broke into Sammy's crib and killed him. The Judge sentenced Tony to 10 years in prison with the possibility of parole in 5 yrs. If he's smart, he'll get out on good behavior in five. Tony had more than enough time to think of those options. At the present moment, he's just happy to be alive...

THE CLIQUE
CHAPTER
Eleven

Everything in the hood seemed really dreary. The rains mist fell from the sky slowly as Kai pulled up to Mona's place. When Kai entered the apartment, she could hear Mona screaming. "What the fuck is going on?" "I can't deal with this shit right now." Mona cried walking back and forth through her hallway. "I can't eat nor sleep and I'm getting really worried Niema. We haven't seen Tony in weeks. "No one has given us any information. Where on earth could he be? Why didn't anyone contact us?"

Mona repeated herself over and over like a broken record not knowing what to think or say. She cried at every sound of the phone or doorbell in her large 2- bedroom apartment in Queens. There was no sign of Tony anywhere. He didn't answer his pager, cell phone or contact his sister and that left a big pain in the pit of the Clique's stomach. Niema stated "He'll call us you watch and see. I know my brother, when he's taking care of business. Tony doesn't like any distractions at all. Right now, we all just need to stick together and plan our next move."

When Kai shouted "Listen, we sitting up in here with 2 kilos of coke, 2 guns and $250,000 straight cash." "Now if anything has gone wrong, we need to find out what it is and we need to do it now." Mona yelled

"Word up I hear you talking sis." The girls were hyped up and frightened at the same time. Each of them were now ready to find Tony. As the girls headed for the door with car keys in hand, Kai had noticed that Mona, Niema and Kema were still undressed in there tee shirts and panties. Kai stopped Mona as she ran out of the door. Mona looked at herself and the girls and joked "Yo, would you look at us."

"How the fuck we expect to get anything done looking like this." Niema giggled "The only thing we may pull off dressed like this is standing out on the strip with the hookers and hoes laughing at the same time." All the girls were damn near in tears from laughing so hard. "Well we do look good I must say," Kema said posing in the mirror and smiling at her curves. While the girls showered and dressed laughter consumed the apartment when the doorbell rang.

Within a split second, everyone froze in silence. The constant ringing of the bell soon turned into loud hard knocks. "Open up the door damn-it" Sierra screamed at the top of her lungs. "Mona I know you're in there let me in." Everyone raced to the door taking turns at the peep hole. Once they recognized Sierra's voice screaming from the other side; the girls finally let their friend into the apartment. Just the look of Sierra made the girls want to puke. Her clothes were filthy and the aroma from her body lingered throughout the living room.

Her face looked like a skeleton with ear rings. Her head had gotten so small that her short red hair cut looked shoulder length. Sierra has been this way for months now ever since that sold called man of hers kept feeding her the crack pipe.

119

We got so use to him beating her ass and her forgiving him that it all became normal. But not enough to have her ass around for too long. Sierra started her disappearing acts for days at a time showing up nodding and sweating all over the place. The girls just knew for a fact that she was on that dope.

The Clique tried putting Sierra in rehab several times but she just wouldn't go. After that, no one could help her. She was stuck tricking and hoeing in alley ways and rooftops, anywhere she could think of to get a quick fix, she was there with the quickness. Sierra screamed "What's up y'all?" "Oh y'all ain't gonna speak to your girl! Ooh you look so nice Mona. Where my clothes at? Can I get some damn money?" "I know you holding don't even fucking play with me like that." Sierra shouted from her dried white lips that had built up white mucus coming out the sides of her mouth.

Kai responded "Ok Si-Si, I will fix you up a plate in a minute. Why don't you go and get yourself cleaned up and showered while I find you some new clothes to put on." When Sierra shouted "Listen I didn't come here to take a fucking shower or for you to feed me. I look hungry to you?" The girls just stared at her. Sierra continued "I came here to put you on to what happened with Tony." "Tony!" Niema hollered. "What you mean Si-Si?" "What happened to my brother?" Scratching her peeling face and talking at the same time, Sierra screamed you won't believe this shit here.

Everyone sat down in the living room giving Sierra their undivided attention awaiting the disturbing news. When Niema yelled "Well are you gonna scratch your face off or are you gonna put us on to Tony."

The girls looked at Sierra with disgust as she went into her nodding faze. Sweat dripping off the tip of her nose like rain drops with her body clearly about to fall to the floor. Waking up from a minute's sleep, Sierra began telling the girls how the police had locked up Tony when he was caught in a shootout up in Harlem at Sammy's crib.

Sierra went on and on about how the cops found Vince's right hand man Sammy dead on arrival along with Sasha's uncle Lem and his cousin Reese. She also explained why Tony's been gone so long because he's been locked up for weeks now. and He was sentenced to 10 years in prison. Tony didn't contact nobody because he didn't want anyone worrying over him. Another code of the streets, keeping shit quiet as kept not letting the left hand know what the right hand is doing.

Too many copy cats and snitches out in the world for that! Everybody that smiles in your face ain't your fucking friend that's for sure. Tony gave his goons strict orders in keeping shit quiet about his conviction because he just wasn't ready to face anybody and decided to do his time like a man. Sierra happened to find this information out threw her man who use to be part of Tony's team until he turned Si-Si onto the pipe. Tony also never mentioned to anyone the whereabouts of Mona's new crib. and He Never said a word about the money and drugs he left in it. Tony felt that no one else needed to know of this entity.

Whatever he left at Mona's house was for her and the girls to split. Mona's house was filled with pain and tears. The people from outside looked up and around following the sounds of loud sobs of fear and disbelief.

The girls were in shock and couldn't believe a word that was coming out of Sierra's crusty mouth.

But it was all true. Vince and Tony's Empire was no longer. and Vince will remain in prison for the rest of his life. As far as Tony, he has a great chance of seeing life on the outside of prison again. The game is over and all of the luxury cars, jewels, furs, money and women are all a huge memory of the way shit use to be. Our Men and Women in this day and age are still falling victim to the same traps that were set back then when the real OG's ruled the streets. Of course, you can never knock the hustle, for that isn't the case. These days it's quite a bit of a difference since the 80's and 90's.

Nowadays everyone is filled with so much anger, hate and violence. Don't know who to talk to or trust. Not to say that-that wasn't the issue back then, but at least there was a safe net, some sense of security and a place where you belonged. Back then, you could spot the bad guy from a mile away. Nowadays you can't tell who's who or what's what! Dudes and chicks calling each other bro and sis on social media but tearing one another down behind closed doors. Loving you publicly but hating you privately. That's that fake shit you might want to stay far away from permanently.

Just remembering the days of basketball tournaments, old school park jams, getting fly as ever just chilling, cooling in the shade with a glass of lemonade got damn those were the days. It's just so strange how fast things change and through the years so many lives lost in the thunder when will it end. Back then you took the good with the bad. Today there's more bad than anything and everything around us is turning to dust.

You gotta train your mind to see greatness through all forces of energy. Challenge yourself to be better every day you are beautiful in every way. Self-love starts from within. Take responsibility for your own faults, ways and actions. What you do is a mere reflection of yourself.

Even though Mona and the Clique were rich with jewels, fashion and money; the many smiles of cheer in their young hearts was practically lost to the streets forever.

Money isn't everything people. Although it makes the world go round, it is the root of all evil and you cannot leave this earth with one red cent. The only thing that truly matters is love for your real family and respect towards one another. If you got that, you will find happiness in life. You also have to love and believe solidly in yourself! Know your worth and learn from your mistakes or you will continually fall into the pit of consequence. Live Laugh Love Learn Life...

THE AFTERMATH

CHAPTER
Twelve

It's been a minute since the girls spent a nice sunny afternoon together. Things had changed so drastically. These young ladies came a long way indeed, beautiful and talented with admirable dreams and aspirations. That is something to be proud of in many ways and very commendable. Coming up as a youngster in the projects, where your business is everybody's business. Bitches smiling in your face and stabbing you soon as you turn your back. Fucking your man while claiming to be your friend. Some acquaintances and associates dislike females/males who want to build a better life for themselves; pursuing their dreams and goals. Although people may shoot you down, turn their backs on you, or doubt your ambition, never give up on you.

Once you set up a new path to build and achieve; you start seeing a whole new world out there and that world is so beautiful filled with hope. Some of the most beautiful people live and grew up in the projects. and Some of the ugliest dwell as well. It's not where you come from that makes you, although where you come from helped build that well of stairs for you to climb. It's where you're at deep inside the perimeter of your heart and soul.

Living in the projects has made Mona's life rich beyond confession.

Through all the good times, confusion, beauty and pain; nothing could ever compare to the memories of her childhood. It's like a vessel in your heart that can't be ripped out. As you grow, you either learn from the things you been through or fall victim to it. Growing up in Queens was a blessing although it had its rough times. In life you will never learn anything unless you create enough strength to hurdle your journeys through the struggle. Mona did just that as she shared her stories to the inmates.

Mona visited woman's correctional facilities to shed positive light, share goals and experiences and read short stories and poems of encouragement. "Life is filled with endless memories of the past but you must move forward and choose to live for the future. There are only two roads you can take in this rule of life. Either you stand still in a bubble and take all the beatings life throws at you falling victim to society becoming a statistic like a coward following without a brain." "Or you can stand up and look at yourself in the mirror facing your fears and indecencies building a ladder to success with your blood sweat and tears, holding you up as your strength as you accept what you have and use your mistakes and pain in your heart as blessings to help you reach that higher ground."

"Now which road will you choose?" Mona asked the inmates with a voice of confidence. "We all get one life to live with many chances and ways to live it. What you do in that time is all on you. No one in this world can live your life for you. It is yours and as you were born into this world alone you will die alone."

"So take heed to your blessings in life as well as your surroundings; for there is so much goodness that can come from a bad situation and so much happiness to be gained from pain." Mona continued "I've learned from the best how to survive in these streets. and I also taught myself how to live my way under my own set of rules. No man/woman can control your mind, body or soul unless you let them. So many dark places I've seen scarred but not broken."

"I always believed in myself no matter how hard I cried or how much pain I endured. I lost so many family members that I lost count damn near talking to myself but I'll never give up. Self-love is a powerful thing. Even when you're weak without a quarter to your name, you can never think as if you're broke; always humble yourself and be grateful for the blessings you already have."

"Spent so many days feeling sorry for myself and that day has passed through the grace of god I have been blessed in the name of almighty and given a reason to live again". Mona shouted out loud claiming the victory. Mona never imagined her life this way. She wanted so badly to turn over a new leaf so she decided to make her presence useful as she continued practicing positive thoughts ways and actions taking it one step and day at a time. Mona loves visiting hundreds of young women in prison sharing positive poems and lifting their spirits as they make the transition from being in prison and going back out into the real world. Mona has plenty of family members and friends who have been arrested or sent to prison for many years so she knew firsthand what the system could do to a young soul. It's not easy waking up in a 9x12 cell, staring up at the ceiling with nothing but time on your hands.

Doing time in prison actually helps some people to reflect on their lives as they search for inner strength and beauty and bring forth change in their lives for the better. Mona washed her face in the bathroom looking at her resemblance through the foggy glimpse on the stained steel glass.

Visiting these prisons, taught Mona a lot about survival. The streets were nothing like it. You had chicks in the pen who were doing life with nothing to lose ready to stick you for your last cigarette.

Had dykes in the yard posing like men with their bitches in the cut. That jail shit was tricky, but if you played your cards right you'd be straight. Mona shared another story with the inmates before she parted ways. She had stories for days to share with the inmates she visited monthly.

"Mona met a chick named Jackie on a humble one night when she was selling coke at a strip joint a couple years back. Mona stayed with a hustle or two on deck! She and Jackie talked for hours telling each other crazy stories drinking Tequila shots while watching the strippers swing from the poles. Jackie told Mona how she was in prison for 2 years before she started stripping and had shit on lock selling cigarettes and pills. Jackie got her cigarettes sent to her by the carton. One pack of cigarettes sold for $5 a pack out in Atlanta so she made a killing Upstate. Jackie was a down ass chick from Georgia who got caught cashing bad checks at the bank. She got a lot of juice out in the A through stripping. Meeting Mona was a breeze and both girls Cliqued immediately. Mona had taken Jackie under her wing after one bad night of stripping at the strip joint.

Although Mona was a lot younger than Jackie, Mona was tough around the edges and took no shit from a dude or a bitch. Mona was packing one night when she stopped in front of the diner to get a bite to eat before she headed across the street to the strip club to check up on Jackie. Jackie sold coke for Mona at the strip joint. Practically all the hoes who worked the pole stayed laced with powder every night. Since Mona had kilos to sell she saw the perfect opportunity.

Pulling up to the strip joint, Mona saw Jackie's old pimp trying to take all the money she had on her that night smacking her around telling her she was coming with him until she pays him what she owes him. "Listen bitch, you will say and do what I tell you to fucking do. Where the fuck you get all of this money from." Jackie's old pimp asked as he snatched her purse retrieving all the money that was inside of it.

"I don't work for you no more Mitch give me my money." Jackie said reaching for her purse and crying as Mitch smacked her in the face.

Pulling up, Mona knew she had to do something to help Jackie because that was her girl and her money that Mitch was taking from Jackie in the first place. If she didn't move quick; Jackie would be working for Mitch again against her will. Mona parked her car behind the strip joint and made her way up the block on foot. Walking slowly up the block with her pistol in hand, she could hear Jackie crying as Mitch continued to smack her trying to take everything she had on her that night. Reaching the corner, Mona peeked around and saw a few strippers in their rides along with two bouncers standing at the front door.

Mona could give a fuck who was outside she just knew that-that motherfucker Mitch wasn't going anywhere with her drugs and money. Jackie cried as she tried to break free from Mitch who was still grabbing at her purse trying to retrieve everything inside of it. Jackie screamed "Let go of my purse Mitch get the fuck off of me." Mitch looked at Jackie with rage in his eyes and punched her in the mouth knocking her front teeth out.

Blood just poured out of Jackie's mouth as she fell to the floor clutching the bag Mitch tried to take from her. As Mitch bent down to grab the bag out of Jackie's hand, Mona ran up on Mitch with a fully loaded pistol. "Back the fuck up motherfucker!" Mona snarled pointing the gun at Mitch. "Ha-Ha!" "Oh Shit, look at this bitch coming to the rescue. I ain't scared of no little bitch with a gun." Mitch shouted laughing as he continued to grab at the bag.

All of a sudden Mona's gun went off shooting Mitch in the knee cap leaving Mitch to fall flat on his ass at the curb on the corner screaming his head off. Both Mona and Jackie stared at Mitch as he screamed bloody murder. Then Jackie took a blade from out of her bag ran up on Mitch sat on top of him and cut his face up for knocking her teeth out. Jackie's big breasts popped out of her dress as she bent down digging deep into Mitch's pockets for all of the money he took from her.

Then the two girls ran like hell to Mona's car and pulled off leaving Mitch screaming on the corner. That was the last time Mona saw Jackie before she was locked up for prostitution and possession of drugs. Mona goes in and out about the happenings of her life.

She has been trying for a while to stay on the right path but somehow the streets just keep calling her back. Making these meetings speaking to the youth at prisons really helps her to stay positive. The crowd of inmates loved Mona's stories as she wrapped up her speech before leaving. "It is ok to make positive changes in your life. You are a child of god and you are worthy of a good life.

Your purpose is to find your passion. Your essence is to give great energy. and Your gift is to feed your goals with determination and ambition. Strong people go through an abundance of struggle. Strong people make it through tough times and storms. It takes a soldier to hold their head up high through all trials and tribulations. No fault or sin should never make you feel like you aren't worth another chance to be great. Sometimes people places and things need to be eliminated out of your path in order for you to move forward with your life." The crowd of prisoners applauded as Mona finished her speech at the correctional facility.

Mona felt phenomenal after her speech. Seeing all of those faces light up as they received their new clothes, slippers, under garments, and plenty boxes of can goods and food just made Mona's day. Mona had a plan. She wanted to give back to her community. Mona lived a crazy lifestyle. Her childhood was something she had no control of and her experiences early in life molded her to become the woman she is today. Although it was rough she is grateful for every moment. Every lesson is a blessing, and through every experience good and bad, everything turned out just fine. Beautiful girl full of imperfections torn but not broken! Kai and Kizz picked Mona up from the bus stop after Mona finished her speech at the facility.

The Clique planned a great day to have brunch with all of the girls to catch up on old times and make a few ends meet. Things grew a little slow ever since Tony got locked up. After the girls split the money he left them, they all made a few adjustments and carried on with different goals to better their lives. Kai saved practically all of her money. She went back to school to get her bachelor's degree and she is now investing into a beauty supply store specializing in hair and wigs for cancer patients and women with alopecia.

Kai's been researching and has many life changing opportunities ahead of her. Haven't yet picked the right location for her business, but she is definitely moving in the right direction in doing so.

The reason for the meeting was to set everything on the table about where each girl expects to be in next five years of their lives. Can't deal or slang drugs forever. Smart business moves only come once or twice in a lifetime. It is a wonderful feeling to have someone sit at your table with the same desires and goals as yourself. You might dream a little different, but the hunger to strive a little better feels amazing when your head is in the right place.

Dealing drugs, drinking and sniffing cocaine will never give you the lifestyle you want. The only thing that comes from the fast life is a prison sentence or a spot at the cemetery 6 feet under. The memories of living the life in the mink coats, jewels, fancy shoes and cars will always be what was. Today is a new day a new chance to make a difference a chance to tell your story and an opportunity to seek build and grow. Niema Owns a beauty salon. She's been doing hair for years. Niema can turn some rough edges around real quick.

The business that Kai is investing in will work great with Niema because she can buy and get her hair for wholesale prices working together to make that paper stack just like before but legally. Kizz went back to school while working as a corrections officer. She was dabbling a little here and there dealing drugs with her man on the low moving drugs in and out of the pen but finally put a cap on it for good. Fast money isn't always good money. That fast money will get you caught up.

Your freedom and self-worth is most important. In this world, without change you will have a very bumpy ride. It's a hard knock life living in those streets. The streets don't love nobody. These streets will eat you up and swallow you whole if you don't play your cards right. The secret to changing in the right direction is patience and persistence. You've gotta be patient with yourself. You've gotta make a plan, set some goals, take action and build the ladder to become successful. Self-love is the best love. Nothing is ever handed to you on a silver platter.

You've got to work for your plate at the table. Once you get to your destination, you will feel awesome sitting with confidence. The change is up to you. You are the only one who can make the difference. Rise up to the occasion and win. Sierra on the other hand didn't get so lucky. Sierra's crack habit took over her world.

She was living with her parents for a while until she stole everything in sight that wasn't nailed down. Now, she is living in darkness. All the money that she had is gone. Sierra spent every last dime she had on crack. No shame in her game. She does any and everything she could to get high.

She moves from house to house, staying anywhere she could until she gets kicked out. Her eyes look like racoons staring at you smelling like a bag of garbage. Nonetheless, she will be alright once the system catches a hold of her. The only thing that will keep her sober or rehabilitated at this point is incarceration. After a while, you get tired of trying to help people who don't want to help themselves. The journey of life is meant to make mistakes, faults and mishaps. Without mistakes, there wouldn't be any lessons taught. You live and you learn. Some of the toughest people survived the craziest shit. Real soldiers stand firm through all storms and weather. Your focus should always be hungrier than your distractions. Everything you do is a jewel set for you to use it in a particular way. Your experiences are your greatest teachers.

There is no school that can ever teach you the way lessons in life can. Your power relies in your ability to believe. Big-pimpin never been easy, but Sasha still has the West Side Highway on lock. Tricking became Sasha's chosen profession. Sooner or later no one is going to want that old washed up baggage. Then what? Clean yourself up. Get a trade and some schooling, learn something new and make your time useful. Find your true passion. Feed your brain with a little science or these streets will eat you up if you don't. No matter how hard or how fucked up shit gets. Or how foul people may treat you or hate on you.

You hold the key to your own happiness and success. Happiness is an inside job. You can do anything you set your mind to. Mona has made the choice to become a writer. She's cleaned up her act and she is drug free. She's believed in her ability to write for as long as she could remember.

Her first memory of writing a story was at the tender age of seven years old. Mona's seen and heard it all as a youngster and now characters and stories scream out of her pen. The most gifted people mirror images and experiences from their own childhood that reflects on the ability to inherit great talent. Most may not admit their childhood setbacks but the ones who do become very helpful for many children who can't speak up for themselves. Also helpful for all the women who are too scared to talk about being abused or attacked. and All the women and men who are too embarrassed to admit they have a drug addiction or problem. All of these issues are happening in our lives as we read, work, watch television and speak. You can help so many people by speaking of your own mishaps, faults and experiences.

"What a lovely day!" Mona smiled as the girls pulled up at Sammy's Restaurant in City Island. Hugging one another smiling and joking as they ordered their drinks and food. Mona interrupts everybody and says "Ok look, we had a long run with this drug shit, a long run with getting away with felonies, drug and gun charges, beating the system with the bread we kept in our safes cutting up thousands of kilos of cocaine. Bussing off shots feeding the community with this poison." "Let's talk some real shit." Mona said with her hands in the air.

"Let's talk some positive shit. Let's come to the table with self- worth self- esteem and self -confidence. Let's motivate each other to do better than we did yesterday. I don't go up to those jails to just talk out of my ass. I'm doing this shit to make a difference in their lives as well as my own." "If you really truly want to make a change, you must start with yourself.

134

Improving your own ways and actions giving light to all the darkness around us. This money we made came through dirty choices and decisions but we can use it to better the lives of others as well as our own."

'Who's down to set a new path for the Clique?" Mona took out her gun and sat it on the table. "Yo! I'm done living like this. I walk around with a gun for protection from these streets. I'm tired of being strapped walking around watching my back. This lifestyle is whack and I'm ready to move forward to something bigger and better. My best friend Tony is doing 10yrs in prison and I'm starting to see things much clearer now. God is working on me and I am ready to make all of my goals dreams and aspirations come true." Mona whispered to the girls as she waited for them to place their guns on the table as well.

"The only thing you are about to make come true is a gun charge, if you don't get that fucking gun off the table." We all will be going in thirsty and hungry as fuck." Kai snarled rolling her eyes at Mona waiting for her to get her gun off of the table. All the girls bussed out laughing as they ate their salad. "Oh my bad!" Mona laughed at her sister with a devilish grin. "You gotta start somewhere Damn it. Y'all know what I mean shit." "Where's the fucking drinks?" The girls remained quiet taking heed to what Mona was saying.

The best days of your life is when you can share it with the right people. Never give up on yourself. You are the strongest person you've got. Your strength moves mountains. A setback is a setup for a major come back remember that. Mona went on to be a positive public speaker to children in youth and made donations to woman at correctional facilities.

She made her biggest dream come true publishing her first short story novel. The best things in life are free which is love, patience, understanding, strength, courage and the wisdom to know the difference. Your own mirror of reflections is priceless. To be a Boss is to be a risk taker, a leader and a go getter. The world would open up so many doors for you if you just believe in yourself. No matter what obstacles you face, good, bad, or ugly. Nothing is strong enough to keep you down. Get up after every fall and rise after every dilemma. It's up to you to make it through. Like they say, if you don't have any haters, you are not doing something right. So let the haters hate, talk shit and say what they want as long as they spell your name right. The real fight is within. Inner strength and peace can walk away from any battle. You have the power to remove anything that is toxic away from your life. Anything that hinders your ability to rise, get rid of it. Anyone who has a problem with your smiles and grace, kick them to the curb. Let nothing or no one dim the light that shines from within. No matter what you go through there is always going to be a bright light at the end of all struggle. Only the strong survive and thrive through the archives. So never give up on yourself.

The girls ordered stuffed lobsters, jumbo shrimp, king crab legs and plenty drinks celebrating their independence and freedom. Through all the drama, the violence and the pain, the Clique was just happy to be at peace with one another. They just wanted to enjoy life for the moment with no worries. True friends and family understand your pain, love you whether happy or insane, be a shoulder through hard times when it rains and give you room to learn and grow while you maintain.

All you heard was laughter, jokes and smiles at their table. All the problems of the world were gone. As long as they had each other, nothing else mattered...

Paving the Way

Lift your head up high girls. Be strong girls. Grab a hold of your life, deepest dreams, goals and emotions. Everything will turn out just fine. When living in an environment where you absolutely have no control of your surroundings, things can become very overwhelming. There will come a time and point in life when you will have to face your fears and hurdle your obstacles. No matter how hard it gets; you can overcome them all with a little faith and inspiration. Everyday life is a blessing. and Also a test with different answers to many questions we may not understand. If you look carefully and study your soul, those answers will follow through to your heart and shine like a shooting star on a cool summers night. So just believe in yourself and follow your dreams and you too will see the joy that success and happiness can bring.

FIND ME Here

Facebook: Toylin Simone

Instagram: Toylin Simone

Email: toycoworld@gmail.com

Website: toycopublishing.com

—

Toylin Simone

4002 Hwy. 78

Suite 530-361

Snellville GA, 30039

www.ingramcontent.com/pod-product-compliance
Lightning Source LLC
Chambersburg PA
CBHW060122260626
47160CB00005B/1987